THAT
OLD BLACK
MAGIC

THAT OLD BLACK MAGIC

MARY JANE CLARK

WM

WILLIAM MORROW
An Imprint of HarperCollins*Publishers*

THAT OLD BLACK MAGIC. Copyright © 2014 by Mary Jane Clark. All rights reserved. Printed in the United States of America. No part of this book may be used or reproduced in any manner whatsoever without written permission except in the case of brief quotations embodied in critical articles and reviews. For information address HarperCollins Publishers, 10 East 53rd Street, New York, NY 10022.

HarperCollins books may be purchased for educational, business, or sales promotional use. For information please e-mail the Special Markets Department at SPsales@harpercollins.com.

FIRST EDITION

Library of Congress Cataloging-in-Publication Data has been applied for.

ISBN 978-0-06-213547-6

14 15 16 17 18 OV/RRD 10 9 8 7 6 5 4 3 2 1

For Peggy Derryberry Gould,
with endless gratitude for the peace of mind you provide.

And for all those who struggle with Fragile X Syndrome,
as well as the researchers who are working on treatments.
Onward.

THAT
OLD BLACK
MAGIC

PROLOGUE

SEVERAL DAYS FROM NOW . . .

PIPER WAS SIPPING a cocktail, but she couldn't taste it. Her sights were set on the tattered cloth doll. It was dancing frantically, tangled in yellow police tape. The more the doll jerked, the more snarled up it became until, finally, the strangled doll collapsed motionless on the floor.

She watched the pool of blood seeping out slowly from beneath the doll, the wet redness growing, coloring everything in its path except for the knotted police tape. Eventually the tape began to unravel itself, and its snakelike yellow tendrils started slithering toward Piper.

She wanted to get away. Her mind willed her body to move. Nothing happened. She was paralyzed. There was no escaping.

Her fear soaring, Piper tried to call out, but no words came from her mouth. Only a desperate, whimpering sound emanated from deep inside her throat.

The yellow snakes slid closer.

THURSDAY
MARCH 13

CHAPTER

1

MARIE ANTOINETTE WOULD have loved this place!"

Piper Donovan stood agape, her green eyes opened wide, as she took in the magical space. Crystal chandeliers, dripping with glittering prisms, hung from the mirrored ceiling. Gilded moldings crowned the pale pink walls. Gleaming glass cases displayed vibrant fruit tarts, puffy éclairs, and powdered beignets. Exquisitely decorated cakes of all flavors and sizes rested on pedestals alongside trays of pastel meringues and luscious napoleons. Cupcakes, cookies, croissants, and cream-filled pastries dusted with sugar or drizzled with chocolate beckoned from the shelves.

"It's unbelievable," she whispered. "I feel like I've walked into a jewel box—one made of confectioners' sugar but a jewel box nonetheless."

A slight and wiry man dressed in white stood beside her. Beneath his mustache a bright smile beamed. "*Merci,* Piper. I am so glad you are pleased."

"Seriously, Bertrand," said Piper. "It's so crazy. I've read so much about Boulangerie Bertrand, and I've watched the episode that the Food Network did on you pretty much on loop since it aired. So I can't believe I'm actually here in New Orleans and have the chance to work with you." Piper did a full turn, trying to take it all in. "It's not like me to get starstruck, but this is epic."

"The pleasure is all mine," said Bertrand Olivier, bowing slightly. Piper noticed a balding spot on the top of his head amid the bushy salt-and-pepper hair. "I hope this time together will be beneficial for both of us. Would you like to see what I am working on?"

"I'd love to," said Piper.

She followed Bertrand from the display area down a long corridor that led to a large kitchen. Gleaming copper pots of varying sizes hung from pegs on one wall, while another wall was lined with larger stainless-steel ovens. There were two doors, one at the back opening to the outside and another on the far wall leading to an office. Piper caught a glimpse of the desk and shelves inside. Spread out on a long wooden table in the middle of the kitchen were rows and rows of what Piper first thought were large gingerbread men. Closer inspection revealed that the cookie men had been decorated with different clothing in vibrant shades of icing—blue, red, yellow, green, and purple. Their faces had been painted in various expressions: some wide-eyed, others with eyes closed; some tight-mouthed, others with jagged teeth. Each figure had an X marked on its left breast. And a long, thick needle made from chocolate protruded from that X.

"Are these voodoo dolls?" asked Piper with delight. "Amazing!"

Bertrand nodded, grinning at the praise.

"They did come out well, *n'est-ce pas*? These are our cookies-of-the-month."

"I love that," said Piper. "What did you do last month?"

"Nursery-rhyme characters," said Bertrand. "And the month before that, jazz instruments. The cookies-of-the-month have proved to be big sellers for us."

"I can see why," said Piper as she scanned the table. "Who wouldn't want to buy some of these? Wait till I tell my mother about them."

"Feel free to flip through our bakery scrapbook and look at our designs," said Bertrand. He gestured at the cookies on the table. "Try one, please."

Piper could feel him observing her as she selected a yellow voodoo-doll cookie. As she lifted it to her mouth, she paused before biting off the chocolate needle. She laughed.

"I hope this isn't going to cast some sort of evil spell on me."

CHAPTER

2

CARRYING HIS CLARINET case and his straw bag of tricks, Cecil Gregson wended his way through the streets of the City of the Dead. The narrow alleyways were edged with rusty ironwork and rows and rows of tombs. Some of the tombs were modest, some were grand, and most were in advanced stages of deterioration. Marble crosses and statues jutted from their surfaces. Almost all of the final resting places were aboveground.

He squinted as he walked, blinded by the light reflected off the sun-bleached tombs. His heart beat faster as he neared his goal. He wanted to have some time alone beside the notorious tomb.

Cecil pushed the porkpie hat back on his head and groaned inwardly as he came to the bend and saw the people gathered around what was said to be the spot where Marie Laveau rested. Cecil was disappointed that he wasn't alone—disappointed but not surprised. He had heard that more visitors came to the crumbling crypt of the voodoo queen of New Orleans each year than went to visit Elvis Presley's grave. Cecil wondered if he counted as one visitor or one hundred, since that was approximately how many times he came annually to pay his respects.

He suspected that tourists must be disappointed when they came to St. Louis Cemetery No. 1 and saw the run-down Greek Revival tomb. Amassed at the bottom of the crypt were trinkets left by other visitors. Empty cigarette packages, lip-gloss wands, bottles, ribbons, sticks of gum, coins, beads, cards, rocks, and other items that would only look like trash to the uninitiated.

Beads of perspiration dotted Cecil's brow as he found a spot at the edge of a group of tourists and laid his instrument case and straw bag on the ground. He watched and listened as a good-looking, jean-clad tour guide spoke.

"Because New Orleans has an unusually high water table, underground burial often isn't practical. In times of heavy rains and flooding, there have been problems with coffins bursting up through the ground and floating away. Interring the dead in aboveground family crypts is the logical solution."

A florid-faced man raised his hand. "Falkner, these crypts don't seem big enough to hold whole families," he said, gesturing around at the other tombs surrounding the voodoo queen's. "Don't they get filled up pretty fast?"

"They are really very efficient," answered Falkner, the tour guide. "The crypts serve as reusable combustion chambers. The extreme heat of New Orleans bakes the stone, brick, and concrete vaults, quickly breaking down the human remains deposited inside. After a year or two, the tomb can be reopened, and whatever's left is moved to a specially made burial bag and placed at the side, back, or bottom of the vault, leaving room for the next deceased family member to take up residence."

"Eww! Creepy!" cried a teenage girl as she grabbed onto her boyfriend's arm.

"And what about Marie Laveau?" asked another tourist, fanning himself with his baseball cap. "Why is a voodoo queen interred in a Catholic cemetery?"

"Voodoo is a religion, a form of worship brought to the Caribbean and American colonies from Africa through the slave trade," explained Falkner. "But remember: Many slaves were owned by Catholic masters, and they were influenced by that. New Orleans voodoo is steeped in Catholicism. Marie Laveau was a devout Catholic who attended Mass nearly every day. She mixed holy water, incense, Catholic prayers, and saints into the African-based voodoo rites."

"I've heard the term 'hoodoo,'" said the same tourist. "Are hoodoo and voodoo the same thing?"

"Hoodoo is derived from voodoo," answered Falkner. "But voodoo is considered a religion and hoodoo is not. Hoodoo is only concerned with the magical practices of voodoo."

The tour guide walked around to the side of the tomb. "See these X's?" he asked, pointing to the many marks scratched on the crypt wall. "These have been left largely by tourists who've heard that marking the tomb with three X's or spinning around three times or knocking on it or rubbing a foot on it before leaving an offering of some kind will get them a wish granted. I can tell you that it's considered a crime to mark up this tomb or any of the others. I can't tell you if you'll get your wish."

Cecil watched as the tour group moved on. He wanted to yell after them and tell them that he could attest to the fact that Marie Laveau did answer when she was called upon. He knew it to be true.

Reaching into his bag of tricks—past the cigars, the leather cat-o'-nine-tails, and other voodoo goodies—Cecil pulled out a black candle and a pack of matches. Spinning around three times, he lit the candle, laid it at the base of the tomb, and made his wish.

CHAPTER

3

Y OU MUST BE *très fatiguée,* Piper, from your long trip. Marguerite will show you upstairs to your apartment. I hope you will like it."

Piper didn't want to confirm Bertrand's suspicion. It seemed ridiculous for a twenty-seven-year-old to be tired. It was only a few hours' flight from Newark to New Orleans, yet she hadn't slept well, had gotten up absurdly early, and had been too wired to nap on the plane. The reality was, she still hadn't fully recovered her strength after her ordeal in Sarasota the month before. Piper was dying to lie down for a little while.

"Thank you, Bertrand. And how should we do this?" asked Piper. "When do you want to start in the kitchen?"

"Tomorrow will be soon enough," said Bertrand, his eyes sweeping up and down her body. "Why don't you take the rest of the day to get settled? Perhaps a walk around the French Quarter to get acclimated. Early this evening come with us to dinner. We are going to Bistro Sabrina, which is owned by Leo Yancy. We make desserts for his restaurant and will be providing the cake for his upcoming wedding."

"Great," said Piper. "What time?"

"We'll pick you up at seven." Bertrand glanced over Piper's shoulder at customers gathered in front of the display cases. "Now I must get back to work."

Bertrand beckoned to a sturdy woman with a short, stylish haircut and dark brown eyes who stood behind the counter. She wiped her hands on a towel and took off her apron before walking over to them.

"This is Marguerite, Piper. My wife and the love of my life." Bertrand kissed his spouse on her smooth forehead. "I don't know where I would be without her."

"Probably baking for the president or some European head of state," said Marguerite Olivier. "You've held yourself back, Bertrand, to make me happy. You see, Piper, I am the one who can't imagine living anywhere other than New Orleans. I grew up here, and I'll be buried here."

"Well, Bertrand's hardly been toiling away in anonymity," Piper said with a laugh as she shook Marguerite's hand and appreciated the firm grip. "I feel so lucky to have the opportunity to be your guest baker! I'm so glad my mother entered my name."

"We are, too," said Marguerite, fine lines crinkling at the corners of her eyes as she smiled. "Once we looked at the pictures of the cakes you've already done, we were sold on the idea of having you as our visiting artist. We also like the idea of having someone so young and full of ideas."

Bertrand nodded. "Yes, you must show me how you made those sugar sand dollars for that beach-themed cake you did."

"Well, I kinda stole that idea from you, Bertrand!" said Piper, smiling. "I saw the cake you did with the various sugar masks in your book—you know, the one that had all the different ideas for cakes and pastries to celebrate Mardi Gras? I just followed your recipe, shaped the round dollars, and very carefully outlined the little flower thing in the middle. It was making the five little slits that caused the problem. You can't imagine how many of the sand dollars crumbled."

"Oh, yes I can," said Bertrand, grinning. "Because I know how many of those little Mardi Gras masks I broke along the way."

"Ah, I wish I had gotten here a bit sooner," said Piper. "I'm sorry that I missed Mardi Gras."

"Quel dommage," said Bertrand. "But you'll be here for St. Patrick's Day."

Piper looked skeptical. "St. Patrick's Day? Well, sure, but New York is the place to be for St. Patrick's Day."

"Oh, we celebrate St. Patrick's Day in a big way here in New Orleans, Piper," said Marguerite. "Prepare to be impressed."

CHAPTER

4

Ellinore Duchamps puffed and wriggled her way into her restrictive undergarments, optimistic that the result would be worth the effort. Then she donned the full slip and hose. Ellinore was tempted to forgo the stockings, knowing that the day was going to be a sticky one. She couldn't bring herself to do that, though. In her head Ellinore could hear her mama's voice: *A lady doesn't ever go bare-legged.*

She pivoted from side to side, studying her head-to-toe image in the gilded cheval mirror. The girdle could not disguise the steadily increasing thickness in her waist. She raised her arm and jiggled the flab on the underside.

Heaving a deep sigh, Ellinore went to the closet and pulled out a turquoise A-line dress. Its sleeves came just above her elbows and would cover her upper arms. The hem rested at the middle of her knees. At least her legs were still decent, thank the good Lord.

Ellinore stepped into the dress and reached around to find the zipper. That took more stretching and wriggling, which only reminded Ellinore how she wished she could call down to Nettie and ask her for help. After having a full-time maid all her married life, Ellinore had found it necessary to drastically alter things. She couldn't really afford to keep Nettie on even part-time, but Ellinore knew that if she gave up her maid entirely, people would talk. More important, not having Nettie in her life was unimaginable. So now Nettie was paid for one day of work each week.

Nettie had been good about it, saying that she wanted to cut back her work and have more time to spend helping her daughter anyway. Though Ellinore had never said anything directly about the dissipation of the Duchamps fortune, she was almost positive that Nettie was aware of it. Her maid was nothing if not loyal and discreet.

With the zipper finally closed, Ellinore took one last look in the mirror and was glad that she had purchased this dress years ago. Even on sale it had been expensive, but she had worn it many, many times. If something was good, it lasted, and old-money people didn't care about keeping up with trends. The women in her circle wore their clothes for years. That made it easier for Ellinore to cover up the fact that she wasn't the wealthy dowager people imagined.

As the widow of Christophe Duchamps, Ellinore had inherited all his property. Before the Civil War, the Duchamps family had presided over a large sugar plantation along the Mississippi River, with a fifty-room Greek Revival house, gardens boasting trees imported from other continents, slave quarters, a small hospital, and a jail. Christophe's great-great-great-grandfather had even owned his own steamboat. Later there had also been the classic Queen Anne masterpiece in the city, the mansion in the Garden District where Ellinore lived now.

Over the decades, however, the wealth had dwindled as elegantly mannered Duchamps scions took their turns running things into the ground, unable to bring themselves to actually work and doing a grand job of mismanaging funds. Christophe had pretty much finished the job, clocking in at the law firm of a family friend but spending most of his time at his lunch club, at the racetrack, or making visits to various French Quarter watering holes. Finally he stopped the pretense and didn't even bother going in to the office.

Around that time Ellinore had begun to quietly sell off the family antiques. After a while, unhappy with what dealers had been offering her, she decided that she could make more money having a shop of her own. Christophe hated the idea of his wife as a shopkeeper and told everyone that Ellinore ran her little antique store on Royal Street solely because she needed something to keep her occupied. All their friends found it understandable that Ellinore would need to be out of the house and busy. They thought that the loss of her only child had precipitated the foray into the world of Royal Street commerce as a way back to sanity. Ellinore didn't disabuse anyone of that notion.

The plantation and the solid-gold table service that had been used in the dining room while slaves fanned their owners had long ago been sold. Ellinore wondered what those knives, forks, and spoons would have fetched in today's inflated gold market.

Every time she combed the attic or wandered around the house looking for things to bring into the shop to sell, Ellinore hoped she would come across some stray gold serving piece that had somehow been missed and could be redeemed for the cold, hard cash she could so dearly use.

Ellinore straightened her shoulders and lifted her head as she turned away from the mirror. She was doing everything she could to keep up appearances. Nobody needed to know the economic straits she faced. It would be embarrassing and shameful for people to be clucking and worrying about her. She'd rather be dead than have everyone feeling sorry for her.

And though she knew that it wasn't right, she pretended she had no idea that her maid was still spending most of her days and nights working and sleeping in the Duchamps mansion. By feigning ignorance of the situation, Ellinore got exactly what she wanted without looking as though she were taking advantage of Nettie. All the housework got done, and Ellinore wasn't staying alone in the big old house at night. The only hitch was that she couldn't call out for Nettie anytime she wanted something. Doing that would reveal her knowledge that Nettie was working unpaid and would give away her manipulation of her maid's loyalty. As long as Nettie didn't think Ellinore knew she was in the house, Ellinore was only too willing to let the situation continue.

CHAPTER

5

MARGUERITE LED THE way out of the bakery and onto the sidewalk. She stopped at a tall wrought-iron gate immediately next to the shop and pulled a key from her apron pocket. Unlocking the black screen, she turned to Piper.

"This is your key while you're here, Piper. It opens this gate and the door to your apartment upstairs—not that we usually lock both. One or the other is fine."

Piper smiled and nodded as she accepted the key from Marguerite. She was certain she'd be locking both. She was trying to be more careful about taking chances. Her father had been warning her about New Orleans crime, but Piper had written it off to the perpetual worrying of a former New York City cop. Still, she appreciated his concern for her safety. Since she'd lain paralyzed on her hotel-room floor in Florida last month after ingesting poison purposefully fed to her, Piper had been understandably feeling less invincible and more vulnerable. Anything she could do to protect herself was totally worth it.

They climbed up the long, narrow staircase. A single door stood on the landing. It was painted a deep burgundy.

"We lived here when we first opened the bakery," said Marguerite as she opened the door. "Then, after we bought our house in the Garden District, we rented this out for a few years. Now we keep it for guests, or once in a while Bertrand will stay here if he has a special project that keeps him working late at night and again early in the morning."

They entered a small living area, furnished with a love seat and an armchair slipcovered with the same cabbage-rose-patterned chintz. A bistro table and two antique ice-cream-parlor chairs were tucked into the corner next to a door that led to a tiny kitchen with a sink, an oven-stove combination, and a small refrigerator.

"The bedroom and bathroom are down here," said Marguerite as Piper followed her along the short hallway. Marguerite stopped at two panels of fabric that hung from the hall ceiling.

"This is your closet," she said, pulling back the material.

Piper looked in. "Plenty of room for my stuff," she said. "What's that door at the back?"

"Oh, that's a dumbwaiter," explained Marguerite. "We had it installed when we lived here. Before we expanded our kitchen downstairs, sometimes we'd have to use our oven up here when we were busy. It made it easy to send trays back and forth. We haven't used it in a couple of years."

They continued on the tour. In the bedroom an ornate

iron double bed was covered with a pale blue matelassé spread and strewn with white pillows. An alabaster lamp sat on the nightstand, while a small Oriental rug in shades of blue and gold lay beside the bed on the wood-plank floor. The tiny bathroom was dominated by a vintage claw-and-ball-footed tub.

"I love that chandelier," said Piper, admiring the miniature lighting fixture. "It makes this little bathroom look so elegant."

Marguerite nodded. "That came from Ellinore Duchamps's antique shop across the street. She has wonderful things, great old furniture and jewelry. She specializes in the most fabulous candelabra and chandeliers. I bought all those chandeliers downstairs in the bakery from Ellinore. And those candlesticks in your living room are also from her place.

"The fridge is stocked with milk, orange juice, and sparkling water," continued Marguerite as they walked back to the living area. "And the pods for the coffeemaker and sugar are in the cabinet." She nodded at a cardboard box on the bistro table. "The beignets in there are for you, and of course you can help yourself to anything you want from the bakery downstairs."

"Oh, you're going to regret that." Piper laughed. "I don't know if I'll have any restraint when it comes to sampling Boulangerie Bertrand pastries whenever I want. Good thing I'm not going to be here that long."

As soon as Marguerite left, Piper kicked off her ballet flats, poured herself a glass of orange juice, and selected a powdered beignet from the bakery box. She walked to the French doors at the street side of the living room and opened them. A blast of warm air washed over her.

She stepped out onto the balcony. Shiny necklaces of purple, green, and gold plastic beads still hung in the curlicues of the wrought-iron railings, vestiges of the recent Mardi Gras celebrations. Flower boxes filled with salmon, pink, and lavender salvia were affixed to the guardrails.

Piper took a picture with her iPhone and posted it on Facebook. She tapped in a caption: GORGEOUS HERE IN THE CRESCENT CITY!

She scanned the street, noting the signs for a café, a *parfumerie,* a bar, a voodoo shop, and a fortune-teller as well as the antique shop that Marguerite had mentioned. Piper was thinking that it would be fun to get her fortune told while she was in town, when she heard the man's shout.

"Hey, you with the blond ponytail!"

Piper's head shot up, and she looked around.

"Over here, *cher.* Across the street."

A tall, handsome man dressed in a rumpled linen shirt and blue jeans stood on a balcony over the antique shop. His brown hair was tousled, and his eyes squinted against the sun. Piper suspected that he was about her age, maybe a couple of years older. Good-naturedly, she waved back at him.

"I haven't seen you before," he called.

"That's because I haven't been here before," Piper called back.

"Where are you from?"

"New Jersey."

"And what are you in town for?"

"I'm a guest baker for Boulangerie Bertrand."

Why was she telling him any of this? She didn't know this guy. If she were in New York City, she wouldn't get into a conversation with just any stranger she met on the street. But here in New Orleans, it seemed like a natural thing to do.

"Is that a beignet I see in your hand?"

Piper smiled and nodded.

"That's what I could use right now," he said. "Want to meet me downstairs and we can go for a cup of coffee?"

"Uh, thanks, but I'm gonna have to pass," Piper answered. The disappointed expression on the guy's face made her add, "I'm going to take a little nap. I didn't sleep enough last night."

"All right, but at least tell me your name."

"Piper Donovan."

"Welcome to New Orleans, Piper Donovan. I'm Falkner—Falkner Duchamps. I give guided tours of the city. In fact, I just got back from a cemetery tour this morning. Maybe I can show you around while you're here."

Piper laughed. "Who could pass up an offer to frolic in a cemetery?"

As she waved good-bye and walked back inside, Piper thought of Jack. His quick thinking and fast actions in Sarasota the month before had saved her life. Their relationship was growing stronger and stronger, and Piper hoped it would only continue to deepen. She treasured Jack and had no desire to look elsewhere. The last thing she wanted or needed at this point was to get involved with another guy.

She pulled out her phone and began texting: I'M HERE, JACK. IT'S GR8 BUT I MISS U ALREADY.

CHAPTER

6

In Hillwood, New Jersey, Vin Donovan finished clearing the snow off the sidewalk in front of The Icing on the Cupcake. He rested the shovel on the side of the building and scraped the bottoms of his boots back and forth across the cement before pulling open the front door. He inhaled the warm, sweet-smelling air that welcomed him inside the bakery.

"Thanks, honey," called the blond, curly-haired, middle-aged woman from behind the counter as she slid a tray of sugar cookies onto a shelf. "How about a nice hot cup of coffee and a cheese Danish fresh out of the oven as your reward?"

"I'm going to spread some salt out there first," said Vin. "We don't want anybody slipping and breaking their neck."

As her husband cut through the kitchen on his way to the small storage shed in the back alley, Terri waited on a customer who asked to have a simple chocolate layer cake inscribed with birthday wishes. The customer pointed to the cake she wanted. Terri took it from the display case and carried it into the kitchen.

"I hate having to ask you to stop what you're doing, Cathy," Terri said as she put the cake down on the worktable. "But can you please write 'Happy Birthday, Frances,' with an *e,* on this?"

"No problem," said Cathy, immediately putting down the wooden spoon and wiping her hands on her apron. "That's what I'm here for."

Terri watched her assistant pick up a pastry bag full of pink icing and begin squeezing the message onto the top of the cake. Terri had to turn her head to the side and look from the corner of her eye in order to see the words take shape.

"Sometimes it's just so frustrating not being able to do what I used to do," she whispered, not wanting her husband to overhear if he came back through the kitchen.

"I know," commiserated Cathy. "But I'm just so grateful that the doctor says your macular degeneration isn't getting worse."

Terri nodded. "That's the truth. My peripheral vision is fine, and my reading machine is a big help. All in all, I know how lucky I am, but, still . . ." Terri's voice trailed off as Vin came into the kitchen carrying the bag of salt.

"Still what?" he asked.

"Still nothing," answered Terri. "Go ahead and spread the rock salt out front."

"Really," Vin insisted. "What were you saying?"

"Nothing worth repeating."

Cathy picked up the cake from the counter. "I'll go box this, ring it up, and leave you lovebirds to it," she said.

"You know, Vin, I don't have to tell you every single thing," said Terri as soon as Cathy was out of the kitchen.

"True, you don't, but it's a helluva lot better if you do. For instance, it would have been nice if you'd talked it over with me before entering Piper's name in that New Orleans thing."

"And have you come up with every single reason why it was a bad idea?" asked Terri. "I knew better than that."

He frowned, his brow furrowing with worry. "I hope we were right, letting her go to New Orleans like this."

"Vin, let's face it. We are way beyond the stage of *letting* Piper do anything. She's twenty-seven years old, an adult."

"But she still listens to us, Terri."

"Sometimes."

"About important things she does. If you hadn't encouraged her, she wouldn't have gone."

"I think it's good for her, Vin. I really do. Boulangerie Bertrand is a renowned bakery, and she's getting the opportunity to work with a baking master. New Orleans is a magical city, and I think the total change of scene will be good for her. She's been so down since we got back from Sarasota."

"That can happen when somebody has tried to kill you," said Vin.

CHAPTER

7

CROUCHED BEHIND A giant pink azalea in the Duchampses' rear garden, Nettie Rivers waited and watched. The warm, sticky air was thick with humidity, and her knees were paining her. Nettie ached to stand up straight. She glanced impatiently at the Timex wristwatch with the purple band that her grandchildren had given her for Christmas and wondered what was keeping her employer. Miss Ellinore was taking her own sweet time today.

Nettie had a mental list of things she wanted to accomplish once she got inside the old house. She tried to do the big, noticeable tasks like scrubbing out the refrigerator or cleaning the oven or dusting and vacuuming on the day she was scheduled to come. Doing the laundry and slipping it back neatly folded into the mahogany dressers was something that could be done discreetly on her secret days. Polishing what was left of the silver or cleaning out the closets was each also a chore that Nettie accomplished on the days Miss Ellinore didn't think anybody was in the house.

Nettie did her best to make sure Miss Ellinore didn't know that she still stayed in the house more often than not. She liked her own bed downstairs, where she had slept so many nights of her adult life. Though the good Lord knew how much Nettie loved her grandkids, living with them all the time was too much to take. The house was noisy and chaotic. And Rhonda's husband, Marvin, could get nasty when he had too much to drink. Nettie didn't like being around that. Mostly, though, Nettie didn't like Miss Ellinore staying all by herself every night.

Nettie's daughter and son-in-law thought she was crazy for working and not getting paid. They didn't understand. She'd been with Miss Ellinore for over thirty years. Nettie loved Miss Ellinore, and she was too old to start taking care of somebody else's house now.

Nettie had watched Miss Ellinore raise her little daughter while that good-looking but lazy husband was hanging out at his club, betting on the horses, playing cards, or drinking with his uptown friends. Nettie had overheard countless arguments about money, arguments that usually ended with Mr. Christophe storming out of the house and Miss Ellinore silently retreating up to the bedroom. After a while Miss Ellinore would come downstairs again with her face all washed and shiny, acting like nothing bad had ever happened. It was clear to Nettie that her boss had been crying, but Nettie never let on she knew. Miss Ellinore had her pride, and Nettie wasn't going to step on it.

Years ago, after yet another of those arguments, Nettie

noticed that Miss Ellinore began going from room to room, critically inspecting the contents and complaining that there were just too many things in the house. The house looked like the Collyer brothers' mansion, declared Miss Ellinore. She said that sometimes she felt like she couldn't breathe, that all the clutter was suffocating her. Miss Ellinore was also sure that little Miss Ginnie's asthma was made worse by all the dust the old furniture and knickknacks collected.

In the beginning Nettie had felt that Miss Ellinore was being critical of her housekeeping skills. So she had redoubled her efforts to keep the furniture polished, the silver gleaming, the crystal sparkling. She didn't pay much mind when the moving men arrived to take out a marble statue, an antique harp, and a carved Victorian sideboard from the dining room. The room did look better, less overcrowded with generations of accumulation.

But after a while, as more furniture was hauled away, chandeliers taken down, and oil paintings removed, Nettie caught on to what was really happening. When movers carried out the piano that Miss Ellinore had learned to play on as a child, Nettie saw the tear roll down her employer's cheek. It finally dawned on Nettie. The things weren't being sold to lighten up the gracious old rooms. The things were being sold because the family needed the money.

Nettie watched now as the back door finally opened and a figure dressed in turquoise stepped into the daylight. She was carrying a pair of ornate silver candlesticks. Nettie knew from the experience of lifting and polishing them how heavy they were.

Her instinct was to spring up and rush to help Miss Ellinore, but Nettie held back. She observed the woman carefully make her way down the porch steps and across the pea-gravel path leading to the old stable that now served as a garage. It touched Nettie to see Miss Ellinore pause at the stunning magnolia tree, so much bigger and fuller now than it had been when Nettie helped her plant it just after Miss Ginnie died.

CHAPTER

THE DARKNESS OF the interior of the Gris-Gris Bar took some getting used to after the bright daylight out on the street. Falkner paused in the doorway to give his eyes time to adjust before sauntering over to the counter. He took the pack of cigarettes from his pocket, tossed them onto the bar, and seated himself on a stool. As he watched the bartender lumber toward him, Falkner recited the children's verse:

> *"Fuzzy-Wuzzy was a bear.*
> *Fuzzy-Wuzzy had no hair.*
> *Fuzzy-Wuzzy wasn't fuzzy,*
> *Was he?"*

A satisfied grin spread across Falkner's face as the bald-headed bartender rolled his eyes.

"You never get tired of that, do you?"

"Nope. Never do."

"It's not like you came up with the nickname, Falkner."

"Doesn't matter. I like to remind you whence it came, big guy. Now that I've done my duty, I think I'll reward myself with a New Orleans mint julep, Wuzzy, before I head out and give my second tour of the day."

"Sounds good to me," said the bartender, opening the refrigerator and extracting a chilled highball glass. "How goes it?"

"Agony, buddy." Falkner ran his fingers through his hair as if pulling it out. "It's just agony trying to get this doctoral thesis done. I was up most of the night working on it, then up early to give a cemetery tour. Three hours of sleep just isn't enough, man."

The bartender dropped a layer of mint leaves into the glass and tossed some shaved ice on top. "Make any progress on the dissertation?"

"Barely. You have no idea how hard it is." Falkner put his elbows on the bar, leaned forward, and held up his head with his hands. He watched as Wuzzy added a spoon of powdered sugar to the glass and then repeated the layers of mint, ice, and sugar before pouring in a generous jigger of bourbon.

"You're right. I don't know, and I don't want to know," said Wuzzy as he reached for a sprig of mint to garnish the drink. "I barely made it through high school. The only book I've cracked since then is the bartender's manual."

Wuzzy stuck a straw in the glass, put the drink in front of his customer, and wiped his hands on his gold Saints T-shirt. "Let the good times roll, my friend."

Falkner drew hard on the straw and swallowed. "Ah, the breakfast of champions," he said, closing his eyes. "That's one lesson you learned very well, Wuzzy. You make the best julep in town."

"Thanks, man. You would know."

"Do you know where the word 'julep' comes from, Wuzzy?"

"Haven't a clue."

"In the Middle Ages, a julep was something to cool the heat of passion."

"You don't say."

"And, man, did I see something a little while ago to get passionate about."

"Yeah?"

"There was an extraordinary blonde on the balcony across from mine."

"You talk to her?"

"I tried, asked her if she wanted to get coffee."

"And?"

"She blew me off. Some crap about needing to take a nap."

"Maybe she *was* tired. If at first you don't succeed . . ." The bartender's voice trailed off as he picked up a towel and began wiping the counter.

"Oh, don't worry, Wuzzy. I don't intend to give up on her that easily."

Another customer came in and sat at the bar. While Wuzzy took his order, Falkner looked up. Small leather pouches hung from the ceiling. Some of them had little cloth dolls attached. The pouches were called gris-gris, voodoo amulets believed to protect the wearer from evil or to bring love, health, and good luck. Each pouch contained a number of small objects, each with its own meaning. Falkner wasn't much for the idea of a magic talisman, but he knew that others thought gris-gris could bring black magic and ill fortune to their victims.

After Wuzzy had finished pouring the other guy a beer, Falkner signaled him to come over.

"Do you ever worry?" asked Falkner, pointing at the ceiling.

"About what?" Wuzzy looked up. "The gris-gris?"

Falkner nodded.

"It's good for business, Falkner. You know that. The tourists eat this voodoo crap up." A shadow seemed to fall across Wuzzy's face. "No, Falkner, I've got bigger things to worry about than gris-gris and voodoo."

"More problems with your son?" asked Falkner.

The bartender bit at his lip to stop it from quivering. "Got the results of Connor's MRI from the doctor this morning," he said. "There's a shadow on his basal ganglia, whatever the hell that is. Bottom line: Connor is never going to walk."

Falkner put down his glass and stared at the bartender. "Never?"

"Nope. Never. His trunk can't support him." Wuzzy shrugged his broad shoulders, but his face betrayed his sadness. "It's not like I should be surprised, I guess. It's been obvious from the beginning that something was wrong. Connor's been so slow to reach all those milestone things, so delayed with his motor skills. He sat up late, didn't crawl until he was two. He's three now, and he has yet to say a word that anybody can understand or feed himself. But it was tough, man, to hear the actual diagnosis."

Falkner waited for Wuzzy to share the information.

"Connor has cerebral palsy."

"Oh, Wuz. I'm so sorry, buddy."

"Me, too." Wuzzy sighed heavily. "Sometimes I just get so damned mad at Carla for dying. I've been busting my hump, trying to keep this place going while making sure things are covered at home. You can't imagine how tough it is to find good child care and have it running pretty much round the clock. I never know when I'm going to be able to get out of here at night, and somebody's got to be there. Between paying for baby-sitters, therapists, and uncovered medical bills, I'm tapped out, man. I'm drowning in debt I'm never going to be able to repay."

"Don't say that, bro," said Falkner, shaking his head. "That's why everybody is getting together for the fund-raiser on St. Patrick's Day, guy. The whole neighborhood wants to help you, Wuzzy, and that was even before we knew about the CP diagnosis. I'm sure we're going raise a nice piece of change. You'll be able to whittle down some of those bills."

"Great. Then we can hold another fund-raiser after that for the twenty-thousand-dollar power wheelchair the doctor says Connor should have. And another fund-raiser after that for God knows what Connor will need next. It's never going to end." Wuzzy closed his eyes and rubbed them.

"I don't know how you do it, Wuz."

"When it's your kid, you do what you have to do," said Wuzzy wearily. "But if anybody had ever told me that this would be my life, I wouldn't have believed it."

CHAPTER

9

PIPER WAS FAMISHED when she awoke from her nap. She decided to get up, explore the neighborhood, and find a place to eat. She changed into a clean white short-sleeved V-neck shirt and cropped black yoga pants. She grabbed the floppy straw sun hat she'd folded inside her suitcase and placed it atop her head as she walked out the door and down the stairs to the street.

She didn't have to travel very far. The welcoming storefront of Muffuletta Mike's was just down the block.

As Piper walked inside, she surmised that the place was part restaurant, part delicatessen, part butcher shop. One long wall was taken up with a sprawling glass-front refrigerated case housing all sorts of meats and cheeses waiting to be sliced. There were aisles of shelves lined with balsamic vinegars, oils, rice, pastas, salts, and seasonings. Customers sat eating sandwiches at several round tables to the side of the room.

"What'll it be?" asked the teenager behind the counter.

"I'm not sure," said Piper. "What's in a muffuletta?"

The young man recited the ingredients. "Salami, pepperoni, ham, capicola, mortadella, Swiss cheese, provolone, and olive salad."

Although the ingredients were things that Piper rarely ate alone, much less all together, she decided to go for it.

"Okay, I'll have one of those, please."

"Quarter, half, or full?"

"Ah . . . half, I guess."

The teenager wrote up the ticket and attached it alongside the row of other orders above the workstation where an older, heavier version of himself was busy making sandwiches. As Piper waited, she heard the teenager talking to his father.

"So? Can I have tomorrow morning off, Dad?"

"Tommy, I already told you. You have to open the shop for me tomorrow. I don't want to hear another word about it. Don't be so lazy."

"It's not fair," Tommy protested. "None of my friends have to work before they go off to school."

"So what? If your friends' parents want to spoil them, that's *their* business. I don't think it's too much to ask. I work fourteen-hour days, and I need a morning to sleep in every once in a while. You know, this will be your business someday, son. You have to start shouldering the responsibility."

"Thanks, Dad, but who says I even want it? I don't want to be a butcher, making sandwiches for the rest of my life. You're always yelling at me about the way I make the muffs or restock the shelves or mop the floors. I never satisfy you."

Mike shot his son an angry look and then turned back to making the sandwiches.

PIPER SAT AT ONE OF the smaller tables finishing her muffuletta when a man wearing a porkpie hat and carrying a musical-instrument case came walking into the sandwich store. She watched as he slowly went up to the counter.

"You got a muff for me today, Mike?" he asked.

The counterman glanced up. His face was gray and tired, and he didn't look happy to see this particular customer.

"Yeah, Cecil," he answered wearily. "Hold on a minute, man."

Moments later Mike handed the wrapped sandwich over the counter. "How you doing out there today, Cecil?" he asked.

"Not so good, Mike. The tourists ain't feelin' my music, I guess."

"Ah, well. If you ask me, you should try another location, Ceece. Shake it up some. I've told you before, you'd do better somewhere else."

The musician picked up the sandwich and turned toward the front door. As he passed by her, Piper caught a whiff of bourbon and heard him muttering under his breath.

CHAPTER

10

Very early tomorrow morning, the first victim would start his day like so many others before it. He'd get out of bed, stumble to the bathroom, wash, shave, and brush his teeth. He'd pull on his trousers and button his shirt, unaware that he was doing these things for the last time. Then he'd leave his home and go to his business on Royal Street, having no idea of what would be waiting for him there.

With so much riding on the week to come, it was hard not to give in to nerves. The initial part of the carefully thought-out plan would begin in a few short hours. It took one slick customer to act calm, cool, and collected right now.

The needed equipment was already packed and ready to go. It was essential that things were taken care of quickly, accurately, and obviously enough so that everyone would come to the right conclusions.

In a little while, it would be necessary to get into position and wait, just as the sun rose. For everyone else it would be just another brand-new day in the Big Easy, full of promise.

For one poor slob, it would be his last.

CHAPTER

11

AFTER LUNCH PIPER strolled leisurely through the French Quarter. She noticed the people walking along with her. Young, old, black, white, some dressed in sports clothes, others in crisp business attire. Some hurried, most sauntered, yet Piper sensed an air of excitement—or was it the anticipation of delights and pleasures to come?

They were all in New Orleans, a place like none other in America. A city whose residents treasured their food, their music, their architecture, and their ability to live in the moment. Founded by the French, conquered by the Spanish, then taken back under French rule before being sold to the Americans, New Orleans had survived slavery, the Civil War, yellow-fever epidemics, and ferocious hurricanes resulting in the deaths of hundreds, the displacement of thousands more, and the destruction of huge swaths of the city. People who lived in the Big Easy well understood the fragility of life. Piper understood that fragility, too.

She stopped in a candy shop, watching as molten toffee was expertly dolloped onto parchment and fresh pralines were scooped onto a marble slab. Candy makers poured warm batches of caramel and hand-decorated chocolate frogs and alligators. Piper watched for a while, purchased a box of pralines, and traveled on her way again.

As she left the shop, her cell phone rang. She glanced at the iPhone screen. With hopeful anticipation she answered immediately.

"Hey, Gabe! How are you?"

"Fine, kiddo, fine. You got down there all right?"

"Yep. This place is pretty awesome, Gabe."

"Good. Let me tell you what's going on. I think you're gonna like it."

Gabe was not a chatterer. Piper knew that time was money as far as he was concerned. When Gabriel Leonard called, it was because there was the possibility of doing some business.

"I've set up an appointment with a local casting director down there. It's great for you to get a meeting in. Tomorrow at one o'clock."

Piper's mind raced. Smack in the middle of her first day working at Boulangerie Bertrand. How was she going to get up and go without leaving a bad impression on Bertrand and Marguerite?

"Piper?"

"Yeah, I'm here, Gabe. Do you think you could change the appointment until late afternoon—say, around five?"

"Are you kidding? It wasn't easy getting *this* one for you."
Gabe started speaking even faster than he usually did. "Listen,
Piper. These people are casting *Named,* the new Channing Tatum
thriller. Apparently the girl who had the small role that opens
the movie had to drop out. They don't want any of the other girls
who read before, so they're setting up a new session. It's shooting
Saturday, so they're moving fast. They'll be on location at some
big St. Patrick's parade they have down there. They'll have a
helluva time with sound issues, so we're definitely talking a day of
dialogue dubbing with you in post.

"And to top it all off," Gabe continued, "the role you're
reading for is opposite Tatum. It'll do wonders for your reel. So do
you actually think you want to ask them to change your audition
slot?"

Piper immediately agreed. While she was eager to do well
with Bertrand at his bakery, acting was her priority. And this
could be big. Huge.

She'd make it work.

CHAPTER

12

As she walked slowly back toward her apartment, Piper stopped to admire the vintage charm bracelets and watches in a jewelry-store window.

She wandered into a gift shop filled with souvenirs of the city. Miniature Mississippi River paddleboats and plantation homes lined the shelves, along with hats, T-shirts, key chains, shot glasses, plates, and magnets. Piper purchased a couple of postcards to send to her parents and Jack.

Next door a haberdasher's shop displayed wide-brimmed, cream-colored hats designed to ward off the blazing southern sun. Piper wondered if Jack would wear something like that. She didn't think so.

Spotting a large blue sign with a yellow palm painted in the center affixed to a storefront across the street, Piper went to get a closer look. The sign listed the services offered: tarot-card, crystal-ball, and palm readings. Oils, brews, charms, incense, and candles were also for sale.

Piper took a deep breath as she pulled open the door.

Thick damask curtains draped the front window, preventing daylight from entering the space. It took a couple of seconds for Piper's eyes to adjust to the dimness. Then she saw the large figure sitting at a candlelit table in the corner. A heavyset woman dressed in a flowing purple caftan was staring intently at Piper.

"Hi," said Piper, feeling vaguely uncomfortable. "I'd like to have a reading."

The woman nodded but said nothing. She raised her hand and pointed to the chair across the table. As Piper walked toward the seat, the woman's eyes followed her.

"What kind of reading do you want?" asked the woman.

Piper shrugged. "Oh, I don't know. I've never done this before. What do you suggest?"

The woman's eye twitched as she continued staring at Piper. While considering her client, the woman rubbed a large brown mole on her cheek. Piper was close enough to see the errant black hairs protruding from the woman's upper lip.

"I can give you a psychic reading. I am a spirit guide, a medium between this world and the next."

"Whatever you think," said Piper. "Do you use cards or my palm or . . . I don't know, a crystal ball?"

"We don't need any of those. I'm already getting very strong feelings."

"Okay," said Piper, thinking she had made a mistake. This was all so silly. But she'd come this far. Having your fortune told in New Orleans seemed like something everyone should do at least once in life.

"Who is 'J'?" asked the woman.

Piper shook her head, already disappointed. "I don't think I know anyone named Jay."

The woman's eyes were closed now. "It's a female spirit. She's holding flowers in her arms."

Piper watched as the woman sniffed at the air.

"I smell magnolias. Why do I detect the scent of magnolias?"

Magnolias. In Piper's mind they were associated with one person.

"That could be my Aunt Jane," said Piper, startled at the thought of her mother's sister, whom she had loved very much. "She lived in Virginia until she died a few years ago. Aunt Jane spent hours and hours in her garden. She had the most beautiful old magnolia tree."

The woman nodded. "That's the 'J' I was seeing. She says you recently went through something hard. Something traumatic for you. You were very frightened. You couldn't move."

Piper's jaw dropped. How could this woman sitting across from her know about the puffer fish?

"Aunt Jane wants you to know that you must take care of yourself. She says you aren't completely well yet. You still have a way to go."

It was true, thought Piper. Though she had improved in the weeks since being poisoned, her physical stamina wasn't what it had been. Nor was she sleeping well. Piper also found herself anxious and irritable sometimes.

"What else is she saying?" asked Piper, eager to hear more.

"She says you are very talented. There is something you want very much, and you are going to get it."

Piper sat up straighter, the little hairs on her arms rising. How could this woman know about the role she was auditioning for? Her mind raced, and she thought of her father and how he would mock the idea that this woman could have psychic abilities. Yet here she was, telling Piper specific things that she could never have known otherwise. It was incredible.

"Aunt Jane is saying you must be careful. It will not be easy, and you are going to have to give more than you have ever had to give, and it may take you to places you may not be ready to go."

CHAPTER

13

Aaron Kane was suddenly conscious of his wrinkled suit, receding hairline, and ample girth. Working in radio, he'd never had to pay much attention to his appearance. His audience couldn't see him. But now, standing in the office of the program manager and listening to the bad news, Aaron wished he looked better, younger, trimmer. He'd be more self-confident, more able to convince his boss of his worth.

"You're not setting the world on fire, Aaron," said the manager. "Far from it. The ratings are down again this cycle."

"It's just temporary, J.D.," said Aaron with more conviction in his voice than he actually felt. "I admit, we may have spent too much time the last few weeks on police malfeasance, but I was planning on getting off that topic anyway. Tonight I'm going back to Katrina rebuilding."

"Do you hear yourself, Aaron?" asked the station manager. "It's the same old, same old. Some say that talk radio as we know it may be on the way out—and the simple reason for that is that the demographic is aging. You've got to get younger listeners to tune in, talk about things they'd be interested in. Talk about a variety of topics, connect with people, have some fun on the air. You can't keep on doing the same old thing."

Aaron stood silent, his expression sullen. He fought to keep his pudgy fingers from his mouth to gnaw at the nails.

"You're not skating where the puck is going, Aaron. You've got to do something different, something unpredictable and smart, something that makes you stand out from the pack."

"Any suggestions?" asked Aaron.

"That's *your* job, buddy, because, as I've told you before, if those ratings aren't up next go-round, don't count on your contract being renewed."

CHAPTER

14

ON THE FLAGSTONES around Jackson Square, tarot-card readers, jazz musicians, and clowns entertained the visitors who strolled by. Artists, eager to sketch portraits or caricatures, waited along the handsome wrought-iron fence that lined the park. Tourists wandered in and out of shops selling candy, clothing, souvenirs, and ice cream. Charming Creole-style cottages with jalousie-shuttered windows stood flush against the sidewalks.

In the middle of the square, twenty tourists were gathered at the foot of the impressive statue of Andrew Jackson astride a rearing horse. Falkner chose Jackson Square as the meeting spot for his group because of its local color and liveliness. It set the mood for his walking tour of the French Quarter.

"This square started out as a muddy field in the early French colony," explained Falkner. "Troops were drilled here, criminals were placed in the stocks, and executions of disobedient slaves were carried out here. Behind me there are three eighteenth-century historic buildings that were the city's heart in the colonial era. The center of the three is St. Louis Cathedral. The cathedral, with its tall Gothic spires, was designated a minor basilica by Pope Paul VI. To its left is the Cabildo, the old city hall, where the final version of the Louisiana Purchase was signed. It's now a museum. To the cathedral's right is the Presbytere, which originally housed the city's Roman Catholic priests and later became a courthouse. Now, if you'll follow me, we'll go see the inside of the cathedral."

Falkner led the group across the square. Despite the cool linen shirt he wore, perspiration seeped from his body as he stood on the church steps and turned around to face his followers.

"The cathedral, properly known as the Cathedral-Basilica of St. Louis King of France, is the oldest Catholic cathedral in continual use in the United States. It's also one of our most visited landmarks and most photographed sites."

A tourist spoke up. "I heard that the Bourbon Street sign was the most photographed."

"I've heard that, too," said Falkner. "But the cathedral is right up there in the icon department. It makes sense. In New Orleans we know how to party hard, but we also know how to repent for our debauchery later."

The tourists chuckled as Falkner pulled the cathedral door open. "Now we'll go inside," he said. "Since there is no Mass taking place now, you can take pictures. Wander around on your own for a while. I'll meet you out here on the steps in ten minutes."

The group straggled into the coolness of the church. Some

sat in pews to take in the beautiful architecture, the stained-glass windows, the painted ceilings, and the ornate religious decorations. Others strolled down the aisles, admiring the Stations of the Cross, stopping to light candles and say prayers. Falkner was waiting for them when they emerged into the heat again.

"Come on. I want to take you around to the back, to see St. Anthony's Garden," he said.

Delicate bell clangs marked the half hour, and a mockingbird called through the still air as the group entered the garden. The green space was dominated by the tall white statue of a man with arms raised in welcome.

"St. Anthony is known as the protector of childless women and finder of lost things," explained Falkner. "This area has had many functions over the years. It was a place for gatherings, markets, meals—even a dueling ground. Père Antoine, one of the cathedral's popular pastors, used the space as a kitchen garden to feed his monks. He also worked with voodoo priestess Marie Laveau to assist the large slave population, especially women and children."

"A Roman Catholic priest collaborating with a voodoo priestess?" asked one of the tourists, mopping his brow with a handkerchief.

Falkner nodded. "They had more in common than you may think. They both had a desire to heal, sooth, and do good works. They were both very spiritual people. Marie Laveau blended voodoo with Catholicism, especially regarding the saints. Now, if you'll follow me out through the iron gates, we'll travel down Royal Street."

Falkner pointed out an antique shop that once had been Antoine Peychaud's pharmacy. "Peychaud mixed brandy and bitters and served the potion to his customers in an eggcup, or *coquetier.* It's thought by some that a mispronunciation of *coquetier* gave us the word 'cocktail.' The very first cocktail, then, was born here. Thank you, Antoine!"

He pointed out beautiful buildings, carefully maintained, occupied now by elegant stores and restaurants. He called the tourists' attention to the fine oak-leaf ironwork embellishing buildings constructed in the 1800s for a sugar planter. He indicated a small gift shop where Mardi Gras paraphernalia was sold all year long.

"You can go in there later and get any masks, beads, Mardi Gras snakes, krewe costumes, and posters you want to bring back home," he said. "But how about we wrap up our tour by going for a muffuletta, the sandwich that had its birthplace in New Orleans?"

The tourists enthusiastically followed him into the shop. Falkner smiled at each one as they passed him on the way to eagerly place their orders at the counter. Too few pressed cash into his hand. He went to the restroom at the rear of the store and counted his tips. *Pathetic.*

Falkner returned to the front, waited until the last of his group had purchased their sandwiches, salads, chips, and drinks. Then he signaled to the owner that he wanted to talk with him.

"I bring a lot of business to your store, Mike. I'm asking you one last time. Will you show me some monetary appreciation or not?"

"You aren't the only tour guide that brings in customers, Falkner. I'm happy to provide all of you guys with a free lunch, but I've explained it to you before: I'm not going to start paying you to steer business my way. I can't afford it."

Falkner shook his head ruefully. "I'd say you can't afford *not* to, Mike."

CHAPTER

15

IT TOOK THEM a good twenty minutes to drive from the French Quarter to the Garden District. After parking the car, Bertrand, Marguerite, and Piper walked through a gate, passing by rosebushes rimmed with little white lights. Piper held up the hem of her long, flowing cotton skirt as they climbed the steps to the porch of a lavender-painted, double-shotgun-style house. As they entered through the front door of Bistro Sabrina, Piper felt slightly uneasy that Bertrand held her arm instead of Marguerite's.

A willowy, red-haired woman dressed in a sleeveless black sheath looked up from the reception desk. She immediately smiled when she saw them.

"Marguerite, Bertrand, welcome," she said, walking around from behind the desk. "It's so good to see you." She kissed both of them on the cheek.

Piper noticed that Bertrand's eyes swept over Sabrina's figure the same way they had swept over Piper's earlier that day at the bakery.

"Sabrina Houghton, we'd like you to meet our guest baker, Piper Donovan," said Marguerite. "Piper will be helping Bertrand for a while. Her family has a bakery in New Jersey, and she has made some fabulously creative wedding cakes."

Piper shook the woman's hand. "So nice to meet you, Sabrina."

"Wonderful, Piper. I can't wait to hear your ideas," said Sabrina. "After dinner Leo and I should be able to sit and talk with you about them. We're so excited."

"Actually, I want to hear about your preferences and your fiancé's and then envision your wedding," said Piper. "Any thoughts I might have will reflect yours."

Bertrand glanced around the reception area and over Sabrina's shoulder, getting a view of the packed bar. "Business is good, *n'est-ce pas?*"

Sabrina nodded, raising her voice to be heard above the din. "Thank goodness, yes. It's never been better. We're packed tonight, and we're booked solid for the rest of the week and through the weekend. That *Times-Picayune* article a couple months ago really put us on the map."

Sabrina led them through the bar area, which had once been the parlor of the house, and into the dining room. Draping velvet curtains hung from the elongated windows, and fresh flowers in crystal vases decorated the mantelpiece of an exposed-brick fireplace. The walls were lavender, with the ceiling painted the much darker shade of aubergine. The room was cozy but not cramped, with snowy white cloths spread over the tables.

Gleaming silver candle holders of different designs stood in the middle of each one.

As soon as the three were settled into their seats, a waiter came to the table and introduced himself.

"Good evening, my name is Patrick, and welcome to Bistro Sabrina. May I bring you a cocktail?"

"I read that New Orleans is the birthplace of the cocktail," said Piper. "So I think I'll have one. Any recommendations?"

"Legend has it that the first true cocktail was the Sazerac," said Patrick. "Would you like to try one?"

"What's in that?" asked Piper.

"Our bartender makes it with rye, bitters, sugar, and a splash of absinthe."

"Whoa." Piper glanced at Bertrand and Marguerite for their reactions.

"Oh, go ahead, Piper," said Marguerite. "Try it."

Bertrand nodded. "Yes, it's a fitting start to your visit to our city."

Piper laughed. "Okay. Sold. I'll have a Sazerac, please."

When their drinks arrived, Bertrand offered a toast to Piper's visit.

"You've been so welcoming to me," said Piper. "I know I'm going to love it here. But already I have a favor to ask of you."

She explained that she had an opportunity to meet and audition for a casting director. "I know it's not great timing, being that tomorrow is my first day of work and everything," said Piper. "But I'll come right back afterward and work extra hours at the end of the day."

If Marguerite and Bertrand were annoyed, their facial expressions didn't reveal it. They plied Piper with questions about her acting career. She gave them a brief history so far, including the stint on the daytime drama *A Little Rain Must Fall.*

"Oh," said Marguerite, making the connection. "So *that's* how you came to make the wedding cake for the soap star Glenna Brooks?"

Piper nodded. "Yes, Glenna and I became good friends, and when she remarried, she wanted my mother to make her wedding cake. But my mother has macular degeneration and isn't able to manage the intricate decorating anymore. She suggested that I try. She likes that it gives me another focus between acting jobs."

"Smart lady," said Marguerite. "And from what we saw on your Web site, you certainly have a talent for it."

"I appreciate that." Piper smiled. "I do enjoy it," she said. "I guess I hadn't realized how much I'd picked up from watching my mom and helping her at the bakery over the years."

As she sipped her cocktail, Piper had time to study the couple. They seemed very comfortable with each other. She also noted that Marguerite was quite attractive. Now, with makeup applied for the evening out, she looked far different from the plain-looking woman Piper had met at the bakery earlier in the day.

"The food here is as good as at the big-name restaurants in New Orleans," commented Marguerite as they perused the menu offerings. "And many of the desserts come straight from our bakery."

Piper chose a pan-roasted and porcini-dusted chicken over a mushroom, artichoke, and Parmesan risotto, while Bertrand and Marguerite both ordered the sauté of Gulf shrimp in a pancetta, sun-dried tomato, and basil beurre blanc with goat-cheese grits.

Piper turned her head away but managed not to wince when her hosts' seafood was placed on the table.

All three of them cleaned their plates. "Absolutely delicious," said Piper as she put down her fork.

When the waiter brought the dessert menu, she held up her hand and shook her head. "The flight down, the alcohol, the rich food. I'm done. I'm going to take a Tylenol PM tonight and sleep like the dead."

While the dining companions sipped espresso, a tall, attractive man with curly black hair and dark eyes came out from the kitchen. He rolled down the sleeves of his double-breasted white jacket and sat down with them.

"*Magnifique,* chef," said Bertrand, bringing his fingers to his lips and kissing them. "Wonderful meal as always, Leo."

"Thank you," said the chef. He turned to Piper. "And I understand you are going to be making our wedding cakes."

"Cakes. Plural?" asked Piper.

"*Oui,* Piper," Bertrand said. "Sabrina and Leo are doing things a little differently. Their big party will be the night *before* the wedding on the *Natchez.*"

"The *Natchez*?" asked Piper. "Isn't that the paddleboat that takes tourists out on the Mississippi?"

Leo nodded. "Everyone we know will be invited to that. But we want our wedding to be more intimate. The next day just close friends and family will attend the ceremony and a wedding dinner here at the restaurant."

"So you want two cakes," said Piper. "A big one for the boat party and a smaller one for your wedding dinner."

"Sabrina tells me you have some questions for us," said Leo.

He turned and stretched to see his fiancée, waving her over when he got her attention.

"And how many guests will you have?" asked Piper as she pulled a small spiral notebook from her purse.

"About a hundred on the *Natchez,*" answered Sabrina. "And no more than thirty at the wedding."

They discussed cake flavors and icing preferences, shapes and tiers and color schemes.

"How did you two meet?" Piper asked as she continued jotting down notes.

"I was working as a waitress on the *Natchez* dinner cruise, and Leo was one of the cooks," answered Sabrina.

Suddenly Bertrand reached into his pocket and pulled out his vibrating cell phone. He checked the number on the screen.

"Pardonnez-moi," he mumbled as he rose from his chair. "I have to take this."

The others at the table watched as Bertrand walked toward the front of the restaurant. Marguerite shook her head.

"That's been happening a lot lately. If I didn't know any better, I'd swear Bertrand has a lover."

The others were silent, awkwardly averting their eyes from Marguerite's face.

"Oh, don't be so glum," said Marguerite. "I'm not worried about Bertrand and women. Our bakery is his real mistress. He saves his passion for Boulangerie Bertrand."

CHAPTER

16

SABRINA HAD LOOKED as fetching as ever tonight, but Bertrand couldn't stop thinking about Piper. He listened to his wife's even breathing and fantasized that it was Piper lying beside him in bed. Bertrand imagined Piper's long, lithe body snuggling against his.

Marguerite was a good wife, supportive and loyal, but there hadn't been passion between them for a long time. Working together all day at the bakery, talking bakery business at home, the constant togetherness had gradually worn down his desire for her. Marguerite's frequent complaints of weariness and headaches didn't help either.

Marguerite was familiar. Piper, with her smooth white skin and shining green eyes, held the allure and excitement of the unknown.

Sighing deeply, Bertrand turned over onto his stomach. Then he turned to lie on his back again. He fluffed his pillow and tried to get comfortable. He needed to relax but couldn't.

He watched the digital clock numbers change, again and again and again. Finally Bertrand gave in. Realizing that he wasn't going to fall asleep, he got out of bed.

AFTER THE DRIVE FROM THEIR home in the Garden District, Bertrand let himself in to the bakery and switched off the alarm. He thought about what he would tell Marguerite if she woke up and found that he wasn't there. He could tell the truth. He had gone to the bakery. He'd be able to think of a logical, believable reason. Beignet batter left unmixed, a wedding-cake design to be finished, a new recipe to be tried before inclusion in the next book. There was always something that could provide a credible excuse.

The night-light provided just enough illumination. Bertrand walked quietly past the glass display cases and through the salesroom. When he got halfway down the corridor that led to the kitchen, he stopped.

He took off his shoes and lined them up on the floor beneath the door to the dumbwaiter. Carefully Bertrand opened the panel and climbed inside the compartment. He sat on the platform, hunching his compact torso over his crossed legs. The space was cramped, but any discomfort was overshadowed by the pleasure that lay in store for him.

Bertrand reached outside and pushed the button on the wall beside the dumbwaiter. Quickly pulling his hand back inside, he felt the platform begin to move upward. He held his breath, though he knew that the journey could be made almost silently.

Bertrand felt his pulse race. He pictured Piper sound asleep, totally unaware that he was on his way.

Higher, higher. Finally he was at the level of the apartment. Piper was only a wall and a few feet away.

He pushed at the dumbwaiter door, and it opened into the closet. Bertrand swung his legs out and down, landing softly on the floor. He uncurled his body and took a small flashlight from his rear pocket.

Bertrand pushed through the clothes that hung on the rod, pausing a moment to enjoy Piper's scent. He closed his eyes in the darkness and buried his nose in the skirt she had worn that night at dinner.

Light from the lamps on Royal Street came in through the French doors to the balcony, bathing the small apartment in a soft glow. Bertrand clicked off the flashlight, parted the closet curtain, and tiptoed into the hall. He silently made the short trip to the bedroom doorway. Then he stood there, watching her.

Piper's blond hair fanned out across the pillow. Her mouth was slightly open. One leg protruded from beneath the bedcover, her toenails painted a much darker shade than her pale skin. He could detect the sound of her breathing. Soft breath. Warm breath. Youthful breath.

He edged closer. Now he could actually see her chest moving up and down evenly. Funny. Marguerite had been breathing evenly, too, but the rise and fall of his wife's breasts hadn't affected him at all. He'd had no desire to wrap Marguerite in his arms and smother her with caresses and kisses.

Yet it took every bit of control Bertrand had to keep himself from climbing into bed beside Piper.

FRIDAY
MARCH 14

CHAPTER

17

IT WAS STILL dark when Mike arrived at work. He entered through the back of the store and flipped on the lights. As he took inventory in the kitchen, he didn't know if he should be patting himself on the back for being a good father and letting his son sleep in or kicking himself for giving in to Tommy's whining. Either way Mike was exhausted. He wondered how he was going to get through the long day ahead.

He put together a list of the meats, rolls, and cheeses he wanted to get ordered for the sandwiches he'd promised to make for the St. Patrick's Day fund-raiser at the Gris-Gris Bar for Wuzzy's little boy. When asked, Mike had immediately agreed to donate the muffulettas. Poor Wuzzy had a tough row to hoe with a disabled son, no wife, and mounting medical bills. Merchants up and down Royal Street were contributing goods and services to help Wuzzy Queen out of his little boy's problems.

Mike ripped open two cartons delivered the day before. He unpacked the contents and restocked the shelves with containers of potato crisps and jars of marinated mushrooms. Then he checked the meat case, replenishing it with a new ham from the walk-in refrigerator.

He walked to the front of the shop, tidying up merchandise as he made his way to the entrance and thinking how fortunate he was that his own son, while lazy, was exceedingly healthy. Mike unlocked the door. He reached to raise the shade in the front window, then stopped as the door opened.

"Wow. You're here early," said Mike.

"I know, but it's going to be a crazy day. I won't be able to get over here at lunchtime. Could you make me a muffuletta now?"

"Okay," Mike said, turning his back and walking toward the rear of the store.

The customer quietly turned the lock on the front door before following Mike to the workstation and watching as the butcher slid a fat smoked ham back and forth, back and forth across the razor-sharp blade of the meat-slicing machine. Mike caught each thin slice and piled it on the round, sesame-seeded bread that lay split open on the counter. He repeated the process with salami, depositing it on the ham. Next a layer of capicola, followed by pepperoni, Swiss cheese, and provolone.

"Looking good," said the customer, observing from the other side of the counter. "Thanks again for this."

"No problem," said Mike. "We Royal Street folks have to help each other out when we can."

"How many muffs do you think you've made in your life?" asked the customer, setting a shopping bag on the floor.

The sandwich maker laughed. "I couldn't even begin to tell you." He reached for the glass container of olive spread he had mixed himself. Finely chopped green olives, celery, cauliflower, and carrot seasoned with oregano, garlic, black pepper and covered with extra-virgin olive oil, all left to marinate overnight.

The customer persisted. "All right, then. How many muffs did you make yesterday?"

Digging into the olive mixture, the butcher shrugged. "Maybe a hundred and fifty."

The customer whistled. "Business is good, huh?"

"It's all right, but it's nowhere near the place on Decatur. They sell hundreds a day. Every time I go by, there's a line out the door. I gotta find me a way to get listed in those travel guides."

"Location, location," said the customer. "Being near Jackson Square and the cathedral sure helps."

"True," said Mike. "But Royal Street isn't exactly a poor relation in the location department. We're the heart of the French Quarter." He nodded over his shoulder in the direction of the shaded front window. "Plenty of tourists are marching up and down that sidewalk out there every single day. They just ain't necessarily stopping here. No sir, the tourists read about Central Grocery online or in their N'awlins travel guides and put it on their lists of places to go while they're in town. Then they return home and tell their friends, who make it a point to stop when they come down. Herd mentality."

"I suppose the fact that Central Grocery originated the muffuletta also has something to do with it," said the customer, reaching down into the shopping bag.

"Yeah, yeah," said Mike, cutting the sandwich into quarters. "But my daddy made muffs in this very shop, and his daddy before him. Our muffs are just as good as anybody's. In fact, I've had people tell me they're even better than Central's."

Mike reached for the roll of aluminum foil, his back to the customer. As he ripped off a sheet, there was an insistent knock on the front door.

"That's weird. I thought I unlocked that," said Mike.

The customer straightened, wrapping a hand around the leather coil in the shopping bag. "You did, but I locked it again."

Mike pivoted around and stared warily.

"I thought I was doing you a favor," said the customer. "You didn't need anybody else like me coming in this early. I'll go unlock it again if you want me to."

Nodding, Muffuletta Mike turned his attention back to wrapping the sandwich as the customer silently unwound the long leather whip. Slowly, stealthily, the customer edged around the counter, closer to Mike, as the knocking at the front door continued.

"What's the problem up there?" Mike called over his shoulder. "Open the door, will you, and let the guy in."

From the corner of his eye, Mike detected a flash of movement. As the whip wrapped around his neck, his hands shot up. He tried to pry the strap away from his skin, but he only felt it grow tighter and tighter, cutting off his ability to breathe. His face reddened and his eyes bulged as the garrote's pressure increased.

Death by strangulation took a lot of effort. Mike struggled

and fought, but, unable to take in oxygen, he gradually grew weaker. Finally he collapsed, hitting his head hard on the corner of the counter as he fell.

Mike lay motionless on the floor. The knocking at the front door finally stopped. Bending down, the customer unwrapped the leather strap from around Mike's neck.

It was then that the whipping began.

CHAPTER

18

PIPER WAS UP before dawn, determined to get some hours in at the bakery before leaving for her audition. She showered, dried her hair, and went to the closet to pick out something that would be good for the audition. As she looked inside, she got a weird feeling. Were the shirts, slacks, and skirts pushed to one side of the rack? She was almost sure she'd spaced them more evenly.

Looking more closely at the door to the dumbwaiter at the back of the closet, Piper wondered about the exposure it gave her. Had someone been in the apartment when she wasn't there? It was a creepy thought.

Oh, don't be ridiculous, she thought. *You came home from dinner, tired and a bit buzzed from the Sazerac. Who knows how you left things in the closet?*

PIPER WAS WAITING AT THE front door of the bakery when Bertrand arrived. He smiled broadly when he saw her, and she was suddenly uncomfortably conscious of the lacy shell she wore stretched snugly across her chest. What had seemed an appropriate choice for the audition suddenly seemed all wrong for a morning with Bertrand.

"I didn't expect you to be here so early," he said, kissing her on both cheeks. "You needn't come every day to open up the shop with me, Piper. But I am glad for your company."

"I wanted to talk with you about the ideas I have for Sabrina and Leo's wedding cake. I'm really excited about it."

"Wonderful!" said Bertrand as he unlocked the door and turned off the alarm. "You can tell me all about it while I get the beignets started."

As she followed Bertrand back to the kitchen, Piper noticed the large wooden panel with a handle set into the corridor wall. She realized it must be the dumbwaiter that led up to her apartment. It made her a bit uneasy, knowing that there was such easy access.

But she pushed those thoughts aside as she watched Bertrand combine yeast, warm water, and granulated sugar in the bowl of the heavy-duty mixer. After the mixture stood for about five minutes, he added evaporated milk, eggs, salt, more sugar, and shortening.

"Okay, Piper. Would you begin beating and gradually add the flour?"

While Piper followed the instructions, Bertrand went to the refrigerator and took out a huge covered bowl. He dumped the contents onto the floured surface of the worktable and began rolling it out.

"You see, you are making the dough for tomorrow's beignets, Piper. It has to sit overnight. I made this batch yesterday."

Bertrand began cutting the beignet dough into squares. "So," he said, "tell me what you are thinking about for the wedding cakes."

"Well, I thought we'd have three layers—six-inch, ten-inch, and fourteen-inch rounds for the big *Natchez* cake," said Piper as she poured more flour into the mixing bowl.

"That sounds about right," said Bertrand. "What kind of cake?"

"How about a red velvet cake for the steamboat party and a bananas Foster cake for the party at Bistro Sabrina? They're both so New Orleans, right?"

Bertrand nodded. "And icing?"

"Cream cheese with crumbled pralines for the bananas Foster cake and, for the red velvet, my mother has a recipe that she always uses. It's my favorite frosting ever."

"Okay," said Bertrand, smiling. "Sounds good so far. I'd like to try that icing of your mother's."

"I'll make you some," said Piper. "And in terms of decorations, I was thinking about doing fleur-de-lis dotting around the sides of the layers."

Bertrand's facial expression collapsed.

"What's wrong?" asked Piper.

"Ah, Piper, do you know how many wedding cakes I've

decorated with fleurs-de-lis, the symbol of New Orleans? I was hoping to do something different for Sabrina and Leo."

"Well, I had a thought for a special cake topper," Piper said tentatively.

"What?"

"I was thinking about a miniature paddleboat, like the *Natchez,* where Sabrina and Leo met. I saw one in a gift shop yesterday. We could have figures of the bride and groom standing together beside it."

Bertrand smiled again, coming around the table and taking Piper's hands in his. "Now, that's an idea I like. *Très bien!*"

CHAPTER

19

FALKNER GROANED AS he looked at the clock. He was groggy, and his eyes burned from lack of sleep. Why did his dissertation adviser insist on meeting so early in the morning? Falkner dreaded their conversations, and getting together at such an ungodly hour only made it worse.

It wasn't that he didn't have a passion for the subject on which he'd chosen to write his doctoral thesis. "The Origin and Hidden Meanings of English Nursery Rhymes" still fascinated him. The first literature to which most people were exposed often focused on the most basic concerns of children and mirrored the culture's most elemental values.

The problem was his difficulty in coming up with original insights. His research wasn't leading to anything that hadn't already been published. Try as he might, Falkner was rehashing what others had already analyzed.

Forcing himself from bed, he stumbled to the bathroom and turned on the shower. As he waited for the water to heat up, he stared into the mirror. His eyes were bloodshot, and his skin was pale. Spending his days giving tours and passing his nights drinking were taking a toll.

After his shower Falkner debated with himself: Should he shave or not? Would how he looked influence his adviser? Should he be clean-shaven and respectful or sport a stubbled look, the toiling academic totally absorbed in his work with no energy to pay attention to a razor? Falkner opted for the latter. He didn't feel like shaving anyway.

He couldn't ignore his shoes, though. "What a bloody mess," he said out loud.

He wiped and polished the loafers until they were presentable again.

When he stopped at the bakery across the street to buy a bag of beignets to bring to his meeting, he regretted his decision not to shave. The pretty blonde he'd tried to engage in conversation from his balcony the day before was standing behind the counter. She certainly wasn't going to be impressed with his appearance, but he decided to try anyway.

"Piper, right?"

She looked up at him with a surprised expression on her face. Falkner could tell she didn't recognize him.

"We met yesterday. From our balconies?"

Piper smiled and nodded. "Oh, right. Faulkner. Like the writer."

"Same pronunciation, different spelling. It's a family name, Old French. No *u*."

"Well, what gets you up so early, Falkner-no-*u*? I got the feeling you weren't exactly an early-morning kind of guy."

"Man, you're right about that," he said, rolling his eyes. "I have a meeting with my dissertation adviser."

"I thought you said you were a tour guide," said Piper, puzzled.

"I'm doing that to pay the bills while I work on the thesis," said Falkner.

"Oh. So what's your thesis about?"

"Nursery rhymes, if you can believe that."

"I can believe it, but I certainly wouldn't have guessed it," said Piper. "You don't look like the nursery-rhyme type either."

"And what does the nursery-rhyme type look like?"

Piper shrugged. "I don't know exactly, but not like you."

"If you get to know me, Piper, you'll find out I'm full of surprises."

CHAPTER

20

NETTIE LAY QUIETLY on her cot in the cellar, listening to the footsteps coming from the kitchen above her. She could visualize what Miss Ellinore was doing up there. Taking the carton of eggs from the refrigerator, putting a pot of water to boil on the stove, measuring coffee into the percolator. Nettie wished she could just go upstairs and make breakfast for her employer herself. But that wouldn't do. She wasn't even supposed to be in the house on Fridays.

She was glad that she'd spent another night in her old basement room, a place that felt more like home than her daughter's house. She took satisfaction from being there for Miss Ellinore.

But after Miss Ellinore left for her shop this morning, Nettie was going back to her daughter's place. Though Nettie hadn't been there in a few days, Rhonda wouldn't be worried about her. Her daughter knew where Nettie was, even though she didn't approve.

From the time she'd been a little girl, Rhonda had resented that her mother cleaned house and cooked for another family. Nettie supposed, in a way, that had been a good thing. Rhonda had been determined not to follow in her mother's path. She'd been devoted to her studies, and now she had a good job with an accounting firm downtown. Unfortunately, though, Rhonda had made a big mistake in the husband she chose. Just as Miss Ellinore had.

Slowly lifting herself from the single bed, Nettie shook her head as she thought about the similarities between Rhonda and Miss Ellinore. Both were smart, proud, and unafraid of working hard. Neither could stand the thought that anyone might feel sorry for them, though both had had their share of disappointment and heartbreak. Nettie loved them both.

She couldn't say the same for their husbands, though. Christophe Duchamps had been a selfish man, determined to do what he wanted regardless of his wife's feelings or his family's economic peril. Marvin Updegrove was the same way. While Marvin went from one get-rich-quick scheme to another, it fell on Rhonda to keep a roof over their heads. And when Marvin wasn't out scamming, he was sitting at the bar drinking away Rhonda's hard-earned money.

That was another reason Nettie liked to hide out at Miss Ellinore's. She didn't want to be around Marvin. When he did come home, she hated listening to all the schemes, empty promises, and lies.

Still, to make Rhonda happy, Nettie was going there for a visit. She was also going to do some shopping. She needed more candles for Sunday morning, when she and Cecil would get together and praise *le Bon Dieu*.

CHAPTER

21

BERTRAND STOOD BEHIND the worktable decorating a small cake layer. He held an icing bag in one hand and a flower nail in the other. There were three more cakes waiting to be frosted on the counter.

"Want some help with those?" asked Piper. "I love making roses, and I've still got some time before I have to leave for the audition."

"Be my guest," said Bertrand, putting down the flower nail and the bag. "It would be wonderful if you make the roses for me. They are so time-consuming. I like to put at least eight on each cake."

After washing her hands and donning an apron, Piper picked up the pointed stainless-steel rod with a small, round platform about the size of a half-dollar affixed to the end. With a dab of icing, she secured a square of parchment to the platform. Holding the flower nail in her left hand, she applied firm and steady pressure to the plump bag she held with her right. Piper focused on the stream of stiff, pink buttercream icing that oozed from the opening of the piping tip. After fashioning a cone on top of the parchment, she picked up another bag with a different tip. She piped a wide strip as she turned the flower nail, covering the top of the cone. Slowly spinning the nail, she made longer, overlapping petals, over and over. When she reached the bottom, Piper had created a luscious pink rose.

"You are very good," said Bertrand, admiring her work and coming up behind her to put his hands on her shoulders. "And very quick."

"Thanks," said Piper, feeling uncomfortable at his touch but trying not to squirm. "My mother taught me how when I was little. I can practically do them with my eyes closed now. At our bakery in New Jersey, we sometimes decorate things in the front window. You wouldn't believe how many people stop to watch when we make the roses. It's great, because it usually entices them to come into the shop and buy something, too."

"Très bien," said Bertrand, brightening. "We don't have room in our window, but would you like to make roses at that little table in the corner out front? Our customers would probably enjoy the demonstration."

"Why not?" said Piper, feeling relieved at the opportunity to get away. "It could be fun."

She gathered her materials, and within a few minutes, she was set up in the bakery showroom. She repeated the rose-making process again and again, gently sliding the parchment squares with the finished flowers onto a large baking sheet. A small crowd quickly gathered to watch.

"What's the name of that thing you're making the roses with?" asked a woman. "It looks like a giant thumbtack."

Piper smiled, continuing to concentrate on making the icing petals. "It's called a flower nail."

"You could probably kill somebody with that thing."

She looked up to see where the comment had come from. Falkner Duchamps was grinning at her.

Was he really back again? He was starting to creep her out.

Her facial expression must have displayed her discomfort.

"Don't worry," said Falkner. "I'm not stalking you. My dissertation meeting was horrendous. I needed to cheer myself up."

CHAPTER

22

Sabrina Houghton unlocked and pulled back the security gate. She entered the Duchamps Antiques and Illuminations shop and flipped the switch on the wall. Instantly the large space was bathed in glowing light coming from dozens of wrought-iron and crystal chandeliers suspended from the ceiling. Below, gleaming mahogany tables and sideboards held a wide assortment of sparkling candelabra and polished candlesticks. Glass display cases contained smaller silver candle holders, providing purchasing opportunities at lower price points. In the three years Sabrina had been working during the day at Ellinore's shop, she never failed to take pleasure in the sight of the glittering world Ellinore Duchamps had created.

As she pushed her long red hair behind her ears, Sabrina marveled at Ellinore's unerring taste and ability to find beautiful things. She knew she had learned much from her boss. Ellinore took Sabrina to auctions and estate sales as they sought new items to continually freshen the shop's stock. Sabrina hoped to use the knowledge she had gleaned to acquire beautiful objects of her own for the home she and Leo would share after their marriage.

As she continued into the store, Sabrina looked up at a particular chandelier dripping with crystal prisms. The hand-cut glass was faceted with patterns that increased refraction, creating a magical, twinkling effect. Sabrina had fallen in love with the chandelier the moment she saw it at an auction of the contents of an old Garden District mansion. Ellinore had paid handsomely for it even then. Now it hung in the shop for ten times that price. Depending on how generous the wedding gift checks were, Sabrina hoped that she could buy it.

She went to the back room and laid down her purse. When she came out front again, the bell over the front door tinkled.

A man and his teenage son, both dressed in Bermuda shorts and tennis shoes, entered the shop and began to browse around. The boy pointed upward.

"Look at that one, Dad. Mom would love that."

The father looked at the chandelier. "You're right, Russ, she would." He turned to Sabrina. "How much is that?" he asked.

"Fifteen thousand," she said softly.

The man nodded. "It's worth it."

Father and son continued to study the chandelier as Sabrina guiltily uttered a silent prayer that they would decide against buying it. She wanted Ellinore to succeed with her shop, but that chandelier was meant for her.

CHAPTER

23

ON THE CAB ride from the bakery to the casting director's office, Piper noticed two police cars pulling up in front of Muffuletta Mike's sandwich shop on Royal Street. The flashing lights signaled that something was wrong.

Piper was immediately curious but tried to focus on the job at hand. She had to go over the sides of dialogue Gabe had sent her to prepare. There were only a few lines, and she already had them memorized. Though the role was small, the scene would set up the entire movie. It definitely had the potential to be quite memorable.

The part called for a female in her late twenties, naturally beautiful with a good figure. The character, Amy, would be costumed somewhat provocatively. She would encounter the male lead as she was preparing to climb aboard one of the St. Patrick's parade floats. At the end of a short conversation, Amy reveals her name. Later her character would be found dead.

There were a half dozen empty chairs in the waiting area when Piper arrived. She wrote her information on the sign-in sheet and noted that several actresses had already been in. Piper figured she was probably the first one being seen after lunch.

The door at the side of the room opened. A middle-aged woman with a pencil stuck behind her ear walked toward the table to look at the sign-in sheet and glanced up at her. "Piper? Come on in. We're all ready for you."

The audition room wasn't much larger than the waiting area. A young male sat behind a table with a script open in front of him. Piper walked over to the X on the floor, stood on it, and smoothed her short skirt while the casting director took her place behind a video camera set up on a tripod.

"Piper, this is Sam Micks. He's going to be reading with you. Do you have any questions before we start?" asked the casting director.

"No. I think I'm all set," answered Piper.

"Okay, state your name and height, and whenever you're ready."

Piper took a deep breath and exhaled as the video camera began to roll. "Piper Donovan. Five foot eight."

After a few moments, she locked eyes with Sam. She'd never even seen him before, but right now she'd make him the most fascinating man she'd ever beheld. She had to convince the people who watched this tape that she was looking at Channing Tatum.

Piper had the first line. "Oh, excuse me."

"No, excuse *me*," said Sam.

"It's so mobbed, and I'm afraid the float will leave without me."

"I doubt they'd be dumb enough to do that."

"Well, you'd be surprised," she said.

"You should try making them wait," said Sam.

"That wouldn't be fair," Piper said, trying to look a bit confused.

"Well, maybe not to them, but it isn't fair to me if you leave me already."

"I really have to go." Piper turned toward the door in the small casting office as she imagined herself stepping up to one of the colorful parade floats.

"At least tell me your name."

Piper tossed her long blond hair over her shoulder as she glanced back at Sam with a glint in her eye. "I'm Amy."

"You look more like a Leigh Ann to me."

Piper gave him a slightly bemused look as she continued toward the door.

"That was great," said the casting director as she clicked off the camera. "I'll get the tape to the director right away. And would you be available tomorrow and Sunday?"

"Sunday, too?"

"Yes," said the casting director. "We're shooting the tomb scene on Sunday."

"Tomb scene?"

"Yeah, there's a scene where Amy is buried alive. You're not claustrophobic, are you?"

PIPER DIDN'T CONSIDER HERSELF SUPERSTITIOUS, but she was unnerved by the idea of shooting a scene while trapped in a tomb. Imagining herself being laid in a coffin made her chest tighten. She did recognize, though, why the director wanted to take advantage of New Orleans's legendary burial places for the movie. They were fascinating and dramatic.

She looked out the taxi window at the picturesque Creole cottages and brick Spanish Colonial houses on the way back to the bakery. Piper could understand why New Orleans was an attractive location for filming. The culturally rich neighborhoods and diverse locations, from bayou to big city, provided vivid backdrops. There were willing extras of all shapes, sizes, and ethnicities available, as well as state-of-the-art sound stages and plenty of skilled crew members. Piper also knew that Louisiana offered attractive tax incentives to the film industry to bring its business to New Orleans. The city was working hard to earn the moniker "Hollywood of the South."

She should be excited about the opportunity to book some work here. Though she didn't have the part yet, Piper knew that the audition had gone very well. She also knew that that didn't mean a thing. Her look, voice, and presence had to be what the director and producers had in mind, what they envisioned as the perfect Amy for their movie. She hoped the tight shooting schedule would work in her favor. The parade was tomorrow. A decision had to be made quickly. There was no time to drag out auditions over a few days.

Usually she'd be hoping fervently that she would receive an offer, but this time Piper didn't find herself praying for the role. She felt anxious, though she couldn't pinpoint why. Was it too soon for her to be acting again? She didn't like to admit it, even to herself, but Piper knew she wasn't operating at her usual energy level. The doctor had said it was going to take a while before her assaulted system would be back to normal. He'd suggested she might want to get some counseling as well for the trauma she'd gone through. Piper wondered if she'd made a mistake in dismissing that advice.

Her thoughts were diverted as the taxi turned onto Royal Street and came to a stop. The street was jammed with traffic.

"What's going on?" she asked, stretching to see.

"Don't know," said the driver. "The police have cordoned off the area."

A few minutes passed, and still the taxi didn't move. Piper felt herself tensing. She was anxious to get to Boulangerie Bertrand. She'd been gone too long.

She took her wallet from her bag and pulled out some bills.

"I'm going to walk the rest of the way."

CHAPTER

24

ACROSS THE STREET from the muffuletta shop, Cecil sat on a blue plastic cooler. From his vantage point on the sidewalk, he had a good view of all the action. Police officers milled around in front of the old brick building while onlookers craned their necks. Word spread about the murder victim inside.

"Okay, y'all. Keep it movin'."

Cecil watched the young cop urge the tourists along. He liked the kid and the way he usually dropped a couple of coins or a dollar bill in Cecil's opened clarinet case when he passed by on his beat. The young cop hadn't yet had the chance to turn bitter or mean.

Pushing back his straw porkpie hat, Cecil stood up and leaned over to open the cooler. He reached in, took out two bottles of water, closed the box, and sat back down on it again. Opening one he'd laced with some bourbon, he took a deep swig, resigned to the heat and humidity. The month of March was just the beginning of a long season of sweat-soaked days for New Orleans street musicians.

He waited until the young cop looked in his direction. Cecil held up the bottle of pure water in a gesture of hospitality. The police officer walked over.

"Thanks," said the cop, accepting the ice-cold bottle and twisting off the cap. "What a morning."

"Bad news, man," said Cecil.

"The worst for that guy," said the cop. He took a swallow of water. "What a gory mess it is in there."

Cecil looked up expectantly and waited for more information.

"Muffuletta Mike was whipped to shreds, but it looks like he was strangled first. The detectives think the whip was used as a garrote before the killer really got into it. The poor guy was slashed to a bloody pulp, all while the ham and salami and pepperoni were still lying there on the counter."

"Whipped to the red," murmured Cecil. He nodded knowingly at the thoughts that came to his mind. Petro loa, the dark spirits, were the most aggressive and easily annoyed. Red was their color. Pig sacrifice was their appeasement.

The bloody shop and all the pork strewn around were signs of Petro loa.

The patrolman thirstily emptied the rest of the bottle and threw a dollar bill into the instrument case. "Thanks for the water, Ceece. Got to get back to work."

"Me, too," said Cecil. As he brought the clarinet to his lips, he considered the Petro loa's other calling card: It was the whip.

CHAPTER

25

Standing just a few feet from the street musician and the police officer, Piper recognized the man she had seen in Muffuletta Mike's sandwich shop yesterday, the one who'd seemed angry with Mike when he stormed out of the store.

Now she'd heard his conversation with the cop. She looked across the street at the muffuletta shop. Yellow tape crisscrossed the front door. Despite the heat, Piper shivered involuntarily at the thought that the shop owner had made her sandwich just the day before. She wondered what had happened to the poor man. How painful had his death been? His last conscious moments must have been truly frightening.

Her mind slipped to thoughts of what she went through last month. The minutes had seemed like hours as the poison coursed through her system, paralyzing her, blocking her ability to breathe.

She'd been certain she was going to die. Piper had been terrified, but she'd also been angry. How dare someone try to take her life?

Had the butcher felt the same way? Had he put up a fight? In the last moments, did he accept his fate?

And what now for his family and friends and customers? Piper supposed the customers would miss him for a while, but they'd find another place to buy meat and sandwiches. Obviously his friends would be more affected, thinking a lot about him in the beginning, then less and less as time went on. It was the family members who would have to live with the memory of their loved one and his violent death, year in and year out, at every family dinner, at every birthday, at every Christmas, Easter, or other special occasion. Piper wouldn't even let herself imagine how her parents and brother would have taken it had she not survived.

As she forced herself to move on down the sidewalk, she thought of the teenage boy who'd been complaining to his father yesterday, not wanting to come in early and open the sandwich shop. Piper felt so sorry for the kid now. How many times had she whined to her own parents about things that didn't really matter all that much, never thinking that the next day they could be dead? The poor kid must be in horrible pain.

CHAPTER

26

THE MURDER ON Royal Street had come at the perfect time.

Even before the tense conversation with his program manager, Aaron had been consumed with anxiety. His contract was up for renewal, and the ratings for his radio show had been evincing a consistent downward trend. Calls from listeners, which he depended on to stoke the show's energy, were down as well. He wondered if people were finally getting tired of his incendiary taunts and criticisms.

He gnawed at the nails on his pudgy fingers, wincing as he tore one nail so far down that the ripped skin began to bleed. He sucked on the damaged spot and considered what he had been haranguing his listeners about on past shows. There was a wide selection from which to choose. Government corruption, police malfeasance, urban poverty, drugs, the homicide rate, depression and suicide among teenagers trying to cope with the legacy of Hurricane Katrina.

No wonder people were changing stations. Who wanted to listen to that misery all the time? Many nights when he left the studio, Aaron himself felt sad, dejected, and exhausted after pounding at the same gloomy subjects. The show was stale. He needed something new.

When the police scanner on his kitchen table called for officers to proceed to Royal Street, Aaron opened the French doors to the balcony and stepped outside.

The police activity excited him, and he'd hurried down to see what was happening. The first cop he asked merely shrugged and motioned him to keep moving. The next one was more forthcoming.

"Gun wounds are bloody, but they look antiseptic compared to the gashes on poor Muffuletta Mike. The guy was whipped to shreds," said the officer, shaking his head. He gestured to the corner across the street to the musician wearing a porkpie hat while he played his clarinet. "Cecil over there claims it's some sort of voodoo-hoodoo thing. But I'll tell you this much—whoever did it is one mean, angry bastard."

"Have any clues?" asked Aaron.

"None that I'm going to share with you," answered the cop.

"But at least you'll investigate this one, won't you?"

The officer looked quizzically at Aaron. "What do you mean 'this one'?"

"I mean the victim is white," said Aaron.

"Yeah? What of it?" the policeman challenged.

Aaron shook his head with skepticism. "Let's face it. You guys are more likely to pull out the stops to try to find the killer of a white guy. You don't bother as much for anybody else."

The cop paused, biting at his lower lip. Aaron noticed his hand clenching at his holstered firearm.

"I don't know where you get your information from, brother, but you're dead wrong. Now, get on out of here."

Aaron smirked, but he did as he was told. He looked across the street but didn't approach the musician. Cecil would be out there another day if Aaron needed him. He was always out there.

Aaron walked back down the block to his apartment. He went upstairs, drank a cup of black coffee, and scanned the headlines on his computer. Then he went to the bathroom and turned on the shower. He sang as he soaped his fleshy stomach, knowing the subject of tonight's show. It would draw the callers and boost the ratings for sure.

He wasn't even going to get into the racial subject. He had something that was much fresher, something that hadn't been talked to death. Aaron was really going to stir things up when he nicknamed Muffuletta Mike's murderer for his audience.

The Hoodoo Killer.

CHAPTER

27

"I FEEL GUILTY SAYING it after the awfulness down the street, but we've had a good day, haven't we?" asked Ellinore as Sabrina got ready to leave the antique shop. "We sold that console table with the cabriole legs, the settee with the scrolled arms, and the lamps with the Murano glass stems. The table and settee we took on consignment, so we made fifty percent on them, and the lamps were from my house. Those are pure profit for us."

"And don't forget the antique lanterns," said Sabrina as she pushed strands of red hair behind her ear. "Those came from your house, too, didn't they?"

Ellinore nodded. "That's right. They did. Those once hung at the plantation."

Sabrina looked at the older woman. "Does it bother you,

Ellinore?" she asked gently. "Selling things that are part of your family's history?"

"I guess it would bother me more if I'd been born a Duchamps instead of marrying one. It's not like I have children who'd want all the things for sentimental reasons."

Zipping her purse closed, Sabrina was very aware of the pain that Ellinore must still feel at the loss of her daughter, even decades after the child's death. Sabrina couldn't imagine ever getting over something like that. She greatly admired Ellinore's ability to keep going.

"What about your nephew, Falkner?" asked Sabrina. "I bet he'd be happy to have your things."

Ellinore laughed. "I know he would. And it makes my head spin to think how quickly he'd sell everything to some dealer. He's not the sentimental sort, my nephew."

"You sure? Somebody who is doing his doctoral thesis on nursery rhymes would seem to have a gentle side."

"You'd think so, Sabrina, wouldn't you?"

Ellinore didn't add anything else, but Sabrina saw the shop owner's brow furrow and she began twisting the old wedding band on her wrinkled hand. Sabrina had learned that was a signal Ellinore was troubled about something. Sabrina was troubled, too.

"Ellinore, I have a confession to make."

The older woman's piercing blue eyes focused on Sabrina's. "What is it?"

"I did something this morning before you came in. I think I may have cost you money."

"How?" asked Ellinore, pulling her hand away from her gold wedding ring.

"Customers came in and liked the crystal chandelier we got from the old Willis estate. You know, that one," said Sabrina, pointing up at the large fixture sparkling from the ceiling.

"The one *you* love, right?" asked Ellinore with a smile.

Sabrina cast her eyes downward. "I steered them to the less expensive antique lanterns instead."

Ellinore reached out and patted Sabrina's arm. "Oh, don't worry about that," she said. "Who knows if they would have gone for the heftier price anyway?"

"You're the best, Ellinore," said Sabrina with relief, and she hugged the older woman. "All right, I'll see you tomorrow, then? Remember, I have my dress fitting, but I'll be in right after that."

"Take the day off. It's the last Saturday you'll have before the wedding. Besides, I know you love going to the parade."

Sabrina's face lit up. "Really?"

"Yes, really. I'll be just fine here."

Sabrina gave her boss another hug. "I don't know what to say," she stammered. "Thanks so much!"

As Sabrina started for the door, Ellinore called after her. "Do me a favor, will you, before you leave? Attach a 'Sold' tag on that chandelier."

Sabrina stopped and turned, her jaw dropping slightly. "Oh, somebody else bought it?" she asked, trying to keep the disappointment from her voice.

"It's spoken for, Sabrina," said Ellinore. "I want you and Leo to have it as my wedding gift."

CHAPTER

28

BERTRAND AND MARGUERITE were waiting for Piper when she arrived at the bakery. Their expressions were grim. Marguerite's eyes were a bit puffy, and Piper thought she'd been crying.

"Will you cover the front for us, Piper?" asked Marguerite. "Bertrand and I want to go over to the police station and see what we can find out about what's being done to make this neighborhood safer. It's all so terrible."

Bertrand adjusted his big white apron. *"C'est très tragique,"* he said, shaking his head.

"Did you know the man who was killed?" asked Piper.

"Not well," said Bertrand, "but I buy sandwiches from him sometimes. We—how do you say?—we are all in the same boat.

We earn our livings on Royal Street and try to support one another. I buy from him and he buys from me. He enjoyed my beignets, I enjoyed his muffulettas. You see?"

"One hand washes the other," said Piper, nodding.

Bertrand paused as he thought about the expression. "Yes. That is it," he said.

Piper hesitated for a moment before asking, "Are you worried about your own safety here, Bertrand?"

"I would be lying if I told you that I'm not, Piper. But I have a very good alarm system on this shop. If someone tries to break in, the alarm would wake the dead." Bertrand pointed to the front window. "See? I have the security company logo right there where anyone can see it. I hope that makes any intruder think twice. But if that doesn't work, I have a handgun in the office."

Piper turned to Marguerite. "Of course I'll watch the shop. You two go ahead."

"Thank you, Piper," said Marguerite as she kissed Piper on both cheeks. "Come with me. I have a few things I want to go over with you before we leave."

Piper followed Marguerite to the office. Marguerite gave her the code to retrieve phone messages should she be unable to answer because she was servicing customers up front.

"And here is the code for the alarm and keys to get into the bakery. You should have a set while you're here."

"Thanks, Marguerite," said Piper, pleased that the woman was showing she thought Piper trustworthy.

When they went back out to the display room, Marguerite

nodded to a stack of bakery boxes tied up and waiting on the counter. "Sabrina Houghton should be stopping by soon. Those are napoleons, éclairs, and jésuites for the restaurant."

"Jésuites?" asked Piper.

"They're triangular, flaky pastries filled with frangipane crème and sprinkled with sliced almonds and powdered sugar. They originated in France, and the name refers to the shape of a Jesuit's hat. Bistro Sabrina goes through them very quickly." Marguerite pointed to a tray in the glass display case. "There's some in there. Try them."

Piper donned an apron and waited on customers who came in after Marguerite and Bertrand left. She sold two pecan pies, a box of petits fours, and a dozen chocolate croissants. As soon as there was a pause, Piper selected a jésuite from the case and bit into it. She was wiping powdered sugar from her lips when a smiling Sabrina Houghton entered the shop.

"You look so calm," said Piper, returning the smile. "So many brides are going out of their minds the week before their wedding."

"I probably shouldn't be happy, what with the horrible thing that happened down the block, but I just received the most wonderful wedding present, Piper." She explained her boss's gift.

"Wow! That was really generous of her," said Piper. "She must love you."

"I think she does," said Sabrina. "Her own daughter died when she was young, and Ellinore doesn't have any other children. Though she has never come out and said it, I think sometimes that Ellinore considers me more than an employee. I know that I consider her more than a boss. I've learned so much from her, and she's been so supportive of me and Leo and the wedding. Anyway, I'm just thrilled to have that chandelier!"

"That's fantastic," said Piper, looking upward. "If it's anywhere near as pretty as the ones in here, you totally scored. Marguerite told me she got all of these from your shop."

"You should stop by when you have some free time, Piper. I'd love for you to see the things we have."

Piper took the receipt that Marguerite had left on top of the bakery boxes and rang up the figures on the cash register. Sabrina pulled a credit card from her wallet and placed it on the countertop.

"Anything about our wedding cakes yet, Piper? I know we only spoke about it last night, so it's probably too early to ask, but I can't help myself."

"Actually, Bertrand and I were talking about them a little while ago. We have some ideas we're playing around with, but Bertrand still wants to work on it some more with me."

"I'll bet he does." Sabrina rolled her eyes and smiled. "Has he come on to you yet?"

Piper wasn't quite sure how to answer. Bertrand hadn't really done anything truly objectionable, but she definitely got uncomfortable vibes from him. He was too touchy, the look in his eyes too appreciative of her physicality.

Sabrina's question signaled that Bertrand was a womanizer.

"No," said Piper. "He hasn't really *done* anything."

"Give him time," said Sabrina. "He will."

"Why do you say that?" Piper asked.

"Because he's come on to me. Leo would kill Bertrand if he knew. I haven't said a word, because I don't want to ruin their professional relationship. But, Piper, I just want to warn you. Watch out!"

As Sabrina left the bakery, Piper's iPhone rang. It was Gabe.

The director had seen her audition tape and liked it. Could she come in this evening and read for him in person?

CHAPTER

29

THE CROWD AT the Gris-Gris Bar the night before had been better than usual for a Thursday. The place had been jammed—and some of the patrons had taken their beers and drinks in plastic cups out onto the street in front. Wuzzy could only imagine how many more customers he could have served had they not been discouraged by the crowd, passing by the bar to find another.

Wuzzy counted out the money from the cash register and wished again that he could convince Ellinore Duchamps to give up her lease on the adjacent store. If Wuzzy could get Ellinore to agree, he could expand his bar and double his profits. He needed the money more than ever. Connor's medical and child-care bills were overwhelming him. And now there was the latest huge expense on the horizon: the power wheelchair.

He'd approached Ellinore several times, explaining why he would benefit and suggesting that she could find another, less expensive location in the city that would suit her store's needs just as well. While Ellinore had been sympathetic, she told him she had signed a long-term lease at a greatly reduced rent right after Hurricane Katrina. Even if she could find as good a rent elsewhere, Ellinore said she liked being right where she was on Royal Street; there was a steady stream of tourists passing by all day, and she had repeat customers who'd come to frequent her store regularly. Ellinore was sorry, but she wasn't going to relocate her shop just so that Wuzzy could expand the Gris-Gris Bar.

Stacking the cash and slipping it into the bank bag, Wuzzy turned to the computer, called up his financial software, and logged in the deposit.

As he rubbed the back of his bald head, he found himself wondering if the murder down the block would help change Ellinore's mind.

CHAPTER

30

HIS SUPERMARKET RARELY carried what he wanted anymore, so Cecil had gone to the butcher store around the block from the housing project where the owner was now in the habit of saving chicken feet for him. When he got home, Cecil set a pot of water on the stove. As soon as it boiled, he dropped in the four-pronged feet. After five minutes he took them out and rolled off the skin.

Next Cecil pulled out the old black cast-iron skillet that had been his mama's, poured in some oil, and added the feet, frying them up until they were a golden brown. Throwing in some chopped onion and garlic and cooking them until he could see through the onions, Cecil added rice and covered the whole shebang with water. Some salt and pepper, bring to a boil again, put on a lid, and wait till the rice was fluffy and the chicken feet were tender.

Chicken feet and rice had been his favorite dish since he was a boy. He always felt better whenever his mama made it for supper. Cecil needed some comfort now. Muffuletta Mike's death had taken it out of him.

Cecil went in and lay down on the lumpy couch in his tiny living room. He stared at the crack in the ceiling, his eyes watering and his throat sore. He had to rest and tend to himself.

He considered calling his older sister and asking her to make him some of her gumbo. Nettie made the best gumbo in the city. But she had problems of her own, and Cecil didn't want to add anything else to her plate.

He gnawed at the chicken, relishing the round ball on each foot. Having been raised by a Catholic mother, Cecil felt a momentary pang of guilt about eating meat on Friday, especially during Lent. But now that they were grown, he and his sister practiced voodoo, the religion of their ancestors.

After he ate his fill, Cecil licked his fingers and planned what he was going to do next. It was Friday, and that meant it was Chango's day of the week. Chango. A primary spirit force in voodoo.

Chango was the spirit that ruled over fire, thunder, power, and sensuality. He was the dispenser of vengeance on behalf of the wronged. He could help you to defeat your enemies and gain power over others. His colors were red and white; his favorite foods were apples, yams, corn, and peppers. His number was six.

Chango preferred to be kept on a fireplace mantel or on a business desk. Since Cecil had no fireplace, he went back to the stove and concentrated on the small doll he had perched on a small shelf above it. Created out of Spanish moss and sticks, the doll had a hand-sculpted, painted face, was dressed in a red tunic with white trim, and wore a necklace consisting of six red jasper stones.

Cecil understood the significance of the jasper. It was a power and protection stone. Jasper had the ability to influence justice and fair play. It could help to rectify unjust situations.

Singing in broken Creole, Cecil began his prayer, first to Bon Dieu, similar to the Catholic God. Then to his ancestors. Next he prayed to Chango, just as a Catholic needing help for a pet might have prayed to St. Francis of Assisi. Veneration of Chango enabled a great deal of power and self-control. That's what Cecil wanted.

"O Chango," he prayed in English now. "Help me to be victorious over all my difficulties. Make things fair again."

CHAPTER

31

"Jack! Jack, I got the part!"

"That's terrific, Pipe! Congratulations!"

On the balcony of her apartment, Piper stood grasping her iPhone and looking down at Royal Street. It had grown dark, but many of the exteriors of the jewelry stores, boutiques, restaurants, and art galleries were lit by gaslights and lanterns, creating a sparkling and picturesque scene. What a charming city this was!

"I don't know how it happened, Jack," Piper continued, so happy to be sharing her news with him. "Usually I prepare and prepare, but with this there was literally no time. It happened so quickly. This morning I hadn't had a part in what seemed like forever, except for that dog-food commercial, and tonight I've got a role in a legit feature—like one that will have a nationwide release. With one of the hottest actors in the world right now." She paused only to take a short breath. "Okay, it's a small part, but an important one. The movie's called *Named,* and the opening has me meeting Channing Tatum as I get on a parade float. Later he wants to kill me and stuff me into an aboveground tomb in a City of the Dead."

"Charming," said Jack. "Should I be jealous?"

"Of what?"

"Isn't that Tatum dude the sexiest man alive or something?"

"Oh, please, he's married—and you know that was a while ago." Piper laughed.

"That's a relief. I'm sure he's turned into an ancient troll by now."

"Yeah, you're right," she teased. "It's fun making you, the macho FBI agent, a little nervous."

Piper paced the balcony. She told Jack about the audition and the callback and described the details of what she would have to do on her filming days. As she turned at one end to walk back to the other, she noticed the doors opening on the balcony across the street. Falkner Duchamps came out and lit a cigarette. When he exhaled, he spotted her and waved. Piper waved back, but after waiting a few seconds so as not to be insulting, she went inside the apartment. She didn't want him to hear any of her conversation with Jack.

"I'm a little freaked about the being-entombed part, though," said Piper as she went to the bedroom and lay down. "They'll have a camera inside the casket and some sort of lighting in there, I guess, so images can actually be filmed. I won't be completely in the dark, but I hope I don't lose it and get all claustrophobic."

"I see that," said Jack. "It wouldn't be easy under normal

circumstances, but after being paralyzed for real only a few weeks ago, it's natural you might find it extra tough. You just have to remember that it's all nothing but make-believe this time. It's not a life-and-death thing."

Jack's reference to death reminded her of Muffuletta Mike. She told him about the murder on Royal Street.

"It's so weird. I was in his sandwich shop just the day before."

Piper heard a deep sigh come through the phone.

"Jack? Did you hear me? I watched the guy making sandwiches at lunchtime just yesterday, and this morning they found him dead, all whipped up and bloody."

"Yeah, Piper, I heard you. What is it lately about you and trouble? Please, please, don't get any bright ideas about involving yourself in this, all right?"

"You have absolutely nothing to worry about, Jack. Really. I'm down here to make cakes and be in my movie." Piper caught herself. "Can you believe I just said that—'my movie'? Even if I wanted to, I don't have the time to get involved in anything else. And honestly? I don't have any desire to play detective. I've learned my lesson."

CHAPTER

32

I T'S ELEVEN P.M., and you're listening to *The Aaron Kane Show.*
We're talking about the murder in the French Quarter. Do we
have a Hoodoo Killer on the loose? We want to hear what you
think."

The killer listened as caller after caller expressed their
thoughts.

"I think it's a bunch of nonsense, and you're only feeding into
irrational fear. Shame on you, Aaron. The guy was killed, but
it had nothing to do with hoodoo or voodoo. Sad to say, it's just
another murder in New Orleans."

The next caller expressed a different view. "When I was
growing up, my family had a maid who believed in hoodoo. She
did all sorts of seemingly crazy things, like refusing to sweep trash
out of the house after dark because she believed it would sweep

away her luck. She used to lay a broom across the doorway at night so a witch didn't come in to hurt her. She told me once that she had put some of her blood in her husband's coffee so her husband would stay away from other women. Was she nuts? Some people might say she was, but she believed, and so do lots of others. Why couldn't the murder at the muffuletta shop be hoodoo- or voodoo-related? Anything is possible."

Another caller explained, "Hoodoo is folk magic, not a religion like voodoo is. I practice voodoo. I know. Both believe in loa, the immortal spirits of ancestors or representations of moral principles and the natural world, like love, death, war, and the ocean."

The caller paused to take a breath. "For example, Agoue, the loa who represents the sea, is the patron of fishermen and sailors. Think of Catholic saints. Just as many look to those for guidance and protection, hoodoo and voodoo followers look to their loa for advice and help. Believers form very personal relationships with these spirits and want to serve them. They wear clothes of the loa's colors, make offerings of the loa's preferred foods, observe the days that are sacred to the spirit. The loa can possess their devotees. I think it's entirely possible that we are seeing an example with the murder."

The radio show paused to take a break for commercials. When Aaron came back, he made a promotional announcement.

"Join me and the rest of New Orleans in the Garden District tomorrow for the St. Patrick's Day parade . . . and Monday night I'll be at the Gris-Gris Bar on Royal Street. Folks are holding a fund-raiser there for owner Wuzzy Queen's young boy, who has cerebral palsy. Make sure to stop by to say hi and support this important cause."

Then Aaron got back to taking calls. The next one came from a disbeliever of his Hoodoo Killer theory.

"I agree with the caller who said that you're stoking irrational fear, Aaron. The last thing this city needs is publicity about some crazy Hoodoo Killer on the loose. We're still fighting our way back from the devastation of Hurricane Katrina. We want to encourage people to visit our city, not scare them away with some bizarre notion that New Orleans is a place where Hoodoo Killers roam the French Quarter."

But the next caller disagreed with the previous one. "The guy who talked about the loa is onto something, Aaron. The Petro loa are the dark, easily annoyed spirits. They developed because of the horrors of slavery. The spirits couldn't stay quiet anymore. And so the Petro loa, the spirits of action and aggression, came to be. Petro loa are powerful, quick, and symbolized by the whip. The most common sacrifice to them is the pig, so whipping somebody in a muffuletta shop, full of pork products, would seem to fit in with serving their spirits."

"All this talk about the dark spirits is scaring me, Aaron," said the next caller. "What if this murder was committed by someone possessed? And what if this isn't the only sacrifice he wants to offer to the spirits?"

The killer smiled and thought, *This couldn't possibly be playing out any better.*

SATURDAY
MARCH 15

CHAPTER

33

CONNOR WAS CRYING and soaking wet when Wuzzy went to get him from the crib. As he lifted his son, Wuzzy felt the child stiffen, his arms and legs tightening. The limbs hit the bars of the crib, and the boy whimpered.

"Sorry, bub," said Wuzzy, gently rubbing a drenched pajama leg. "You've gotten way too big for the crib. Dad's gonna get you a big-boy bed soon. Something with safety bars so you can't fall out."

Another expense.

Wuzzy peeled off the soggy sleepwear and diaper. Then he lifted the child again and carried him to the bathroom.

"You're getting heavy, kiddo," said Wuzzy. His knees ached as he knelt down next to the tub and turned on the water. He carefully situated Connor on the bath mat to wait while the tub filled. Then he stood upright and studied himself in the mirror. Bleary-eyed and stubbled, he looked almost as bad as he felt.

He hadn't gotten home until almost three. It was now just after 6:00 A.M. The next baby-sitter wasn't coming until ten o'clock. How was he going to make it through the next four hours? If he could get through till then, he could grab a couple more hours of sleep before returning to the bar this afternoon and working through the night again.

He had to get more help at the Gris-Gris Bar, people he could trust to run things when he wasn't there. But that cost money, and he wasn't bringing in enough to hire another bartender as well as be able to pay Connor's baby-sitters. If something had to give, it wasn't going to be the baby-sitters. In the stress and physical wear-and-tear departments, it was easier to take care of the bar than take care of Connor.

Wuzzy detected movement from the bottom corner of the mirror. He swung around and dove in time to catch Connor, who was toppling over, just before his young head hit the floor.

"That's all we need, isn't it, buddy?" asked Wuzzy, his heart still pounding as he lifted his son over the edge of the tub and into the warm water. "You hurting your head. How much can that little noggin take, right?"

Connor cooed and drooled as he sat in the tub. Wuzzy watched his son, his heart filled with love, his brain filled with anxiety. How was he going to do it? How was he going to make sure that Connor got everything he needed? The child care, the medical appointments, the therapies, the special equipment?

Wuzzy was beyond grateful that the merchants of Royal Street and others were coming together to raise money to help him. But no matter how much was raised on St. Patrick's Day night, even if it paid for most of his current outstanding bills, it would be a finite amount. Connor's care and expenses would go on for the rest of his life.

How was he going to pay for it all?

"Come on, little man. Let's get you cleaned up," said Wuzzy, adding soap to a washcloth and applying it to Connor's back. "Rub-a-dub-dub. Three men in a tub."

Tears came to his eyes as he heard his son's mimicry:

"Wub-a-dub. Wub-a-dub."

CHAPTER

34

THE AROMA OF frying beignets greeted Piper when she entered Boulangerie Bertrand at 7:00 A.M. The display cases were full of fresh rolls and enticing pastries. A few customers were already waiting to be helped by two young women wearing pink aprons behind the counter. As Piper entered the kitchen, Bertrand looked surprised to see her.

"I don't expect you to come in on weekends, Piper," he said, his eyes briefly shifting their focus from her face to her breasts. "It's going to be a beautiful day. You should be out there enjoying our *belle ville*."

Piper smiled uncomfortably and spoke very quickly. "Thanks, Bertrand. Really, though, I want to be here. You're never going to believe it—I did get the part. I have to shoot today, but my call time isn't for a few hours. I don't have to make my way down there until then. So I'd love to spend time watching and learning from you, but I'm afraid I'm going to have to take even more time off while I'm here. And I just want to work as much as I can to make up for that."

Bertrand put down his mixing spoon. "You got the part? *Magnifique!*" He wiped his hands on his apron and kissed her on the cheek.

"Thank you, thank you," said Piper, stepping back. "I still can't believe it. But it means that I'll also be on location tomorrow."

Bertrand looked puzzled. "Sunday, too?" he asked. "They shoot on Sunday?"

"Sometimes," said Piper. "They're on a tight schedule. We'll be on a sound stage tomorrow."

"How wonderful for you, Piper!" said Bertrand, nodding with approval. "Marguerite will be so pleased when she hears it."

Piper glanced over Bertrand's shoulder toward the little room at the back of the kitchen. "Is Marguerite in the office?" she asked.

"No, she takes the weekends off to go to the gym, get a massage, and do whatever else she desires. My wife works very hard. She deserves some pampering and time to herself."

Piper smiled. "That's smart, Bertrand." But she found herself wishing that Bertrand's wife were with them in the bakery.

PIPER HELPED OUT AT THE counter as a steady stream of customers came in throughout the morning. They bought bags of powdered beignets, French almond croissants, and rings of buttery pastry with praline filling and caramel icing sprinkled with sweet southern pecans. Piper noticed that the voodoo cookies were also big sellers. She was about to go to the kitchen to ask Bertrand if he wanted her to try her hand at decorating more cookies when she noticed three men enter the store together. One of them came to the counter and asked to see Bertrand.

"I'll get him for you," said Piper.

Bertrand immediately came out to the front and shook hands with the men. They chatted for a few minutes before he led them back to his office. After about twenty minutes, the men emerged. Piper could hear Bertrand's instruction to them before he turned back to the kitchen.

"Go ahead, make yourselves at home and get whatever you need. If you have any questions, please don't hesitate to ask."

As she continued to wait on customers, Piper was aware of the men's activity. One took measurements of the space. Another took pictures of the room—the chandeliers, the display cases, and their contents. The third, a man wearing a red shirt, watched intently as the customers ordered and paid for their baked goods. Piper noticed that the man engaged several customers in conversation as they left the store.

What was he talking with them about?

She edged her way down to the end of the counter, closer to the front door. She was able to catch snippets of conversation.

"If this bakery were somewhere else, would you still patronize it?" asked the man in the red shirt.

"Sure, if it had the same quality stuff that this one does," answered the customer. "I'm only a tourist, but I've been here every morning during the trip. If this were near my town, I'd be there all the time."

CHAPTER

35

"WHEN THE SAINTS Go Marching In" could be counted on to collect a crowd on Royal Street. Cecil nodded appreciatively at the onlookers as they applauded when he finished playing. Taking the clarinet from his mouth, he watched the dollar bills pile up in his instrument case.

It was time to take a little break. He reached down and opened his cooler. As he took out a bottle of water mixed with bourbon, Cecil felt a tap on his shoulder. A gangly young man with acne on his face stood beside him.

"Hey, I'm Mike's son," said the teenager.

"I know who you are, Tommy," said Cecil, standing up and offering his hand. "Sorry 'bout your daddy."

"Thank you," said Tommy. "I came because my dad always

liked jazz funerals. My mom and I wanted to know if you could organize one for my father."

Cecil considered the request. When a respected fellow musician died, other New Orleans musicians played in the funeral procession from the church, the funeral home, or the home of the deceased to the cemetery. It was a sign of respect. Jazz funerals were sometimes done for young people, too. No matter the circumstances, when someone young died, it was always a tragedy. Prominent members of the community also qualified. Cecil wasn't quite sure if Muffuletta Mike would be considered a prominent citizen of New Orleans, but if his family was willing to pay, Cecil would be able to round up musicians always hungry for gigs.

"When's the funeral?" he asked.

"Tuesday. My mother wants to get it over with, but the priest won't do a funeral Mass on Sunday, and Monday is St. Patrick's Day."

"St. Patrick's Day would be bad," agreed Cecil. "It'd be real hard getting men together to play then. So many have gigs in bars and restaurants. How y'all doin' anyway?"

The teenager shrugged. "My ma's doing what she has to do, I guess. She wants to reopen the shop as soon as possible," he said glumly.

"Who gonna run it?" asked Cecil.

"She is, and I'm going to help her."

Based on some of the conversations between father and son that Cecil had overheard in the sandwich shop, he was pretty sure the kid was none too happy about the prospect. The kid would have to suck it up and get over it. Life was tough, and you had to do what you had to do.

"Well, tell your mama that I'll get some boys together," said Cecil, pushing his hat back on his head. "Where the funeral at?"

"Our Lady of Guadalupe. Tuesday morning at ten."

As the young man walked away, Cecil knew that it was the right thing to be accommodating. The kid and his mother were in charge now. He wanted to stay on their good sides. He didn't need anyone else telling him to move away from his lucky spot.

Muffuletta Mike had been wrong to do that.

CHAPTER

36

EVEN THOUGH IT was part of his job to create goodwill for the radio station and hopefully boost ratings with public appearances, Aaron enjoyed his role as a local celebrity. Much of his free time was spent attending fund-raisers, acting as master of ceremonies at charity auctions, or attending the dedication of new buildings. This morning he would be wielding one of the kissing canes at the St. Patrick's parade. Held the Saturday before the actual feast of St. Patrick—so that work didn't keep people from attending the parade in the Irish Channel—the parade was always a colorful and huge event.

Traffic moved slowly as he drove down Royal Street. Passing the Gris-Gris Bar, Aaron remembered that Monday night, the real St. Patrick's Day, he had committed to emceeing the fund-raiser for the bartender's kid. It was a worthwhile cause, and Aaron looked forward to it. The green beer would be flowing.

He turned his head to look at the other side of the street. There was actually a line forming in front of Boulangerie Bertrand. Aaron wasn't too happy to see it. A couple of weeks earlier, Bertrand had dropped his *Aaron Kane Show* sponsorship. The program manager had really grumbled about that. But maybe, if this new series of hoodoo-themed shows took off as Aaron prayed they would, the bakery would get back on board.

The taxi traveled farther down the block, passing Muffuletta Mike's. The shades were drawn, and the yellow police tape still obstructed the door. The building looked eerie and forlorn. But the stream of people barely seemed to notice as they passed, and Cecil in his porkpie hat continued playing his clarinet on the sidewalk.

Aaron made a mental note to talk to the musician. It would be interesting to get his take on the whole hoodoo thing. In fact, if the guy was colorful and interesting enough, maybe Aaron would ask him if he'd like to be a guest on the show one night.

CHAPTER

37

Piper stood in front of Boulangerie Bertrand frantically trying to wave down a taxi. Each one that went by was already occupied.

She couldn't be late getting to the parade staging area. Piper thought she'd left plenty of time to get to the place where she was to meet the film crew. She hadn't accounted for the fact that she wouldn't be able to get a ride.

She started to walk down Royal Street. If she could get over to Canal Street, she might stand a better chance of finding a cab. But when she reached the wide thoroughfare, she had no luck.

Her face twisted in a worried frown, Piper stood at the side of the street straining to catch a glimpse of any taxi in the distance. There weren't any.

What was she going to do?

"Hey, *cher*. Need a lift?"

Piper looked over at the dusty, moss-colored sedan that had pulled up beside her. The car windows were open. A middle-aged man wearing a green T-shirt was behind the steering wheel.

"I need to get to Felicity and Magazine," said Piper. "But I can't find a cab."

"And you ain't *gonna* find one," said the driver. "This is one of the busiest days of the year, *cher*. But I'm goin' over that way to see the parade myself. I'll give you a ride if you want. I don't know if we'll be able to get to Felicity and Magazine, but I'll drop you off as close as I can."

Piper quickly calculated whether it was wise to accept the stranger's offer. It probably wasn't. But she was desperate. She reached for the handle on the car door and got inside.

Her parents and Jack would die if they knew what she was doing.

CHAPTER

38

FALKNER HURRIED BACK to his apartment after finishing his morning tour of the Garden District. He was determined to make some progress on his thesis. Every day he woke up planning to get something written. Today he was actually going to do it. No matter that he was going to miss the St. Patrick's parade. He had partied hard enough at Mardi Gras. That was part of his problem. He was always finding a good reason to party. He knew he had to practice at least some discipline.

Falkner sat at his desk and switched on the computer. It helped to have a plan. He was going to tackle one of the oldest and best-known English nursery rhymes. He typed in the first verse.

Pat-a-cake, pat-a-cake, baker's man.
Bake me a cake just as fast as you can.
Pat it and roll it and mark it with a "B."
And put it in the oven for Baby and me.

Falkner continued to type, noting that parents and caregivers often replaced the "B" and "Baby" in the last two lines with their child's first initial and first name when reciting or reading the rhyme.

Patty cake, patty cake, baker's man
Bake me a cake as fast as you can
Roll it up, roll it up
And throw it in a pan!
Patty cake, patty cake, baker's man.

Falkner described how the rhyme had developed to be accompanied with elaborate clapping patterns, teaching children hand-eye coordination and rhythm.

Patty cake, patty cake, baker's man
Bake me a cake as fast as you can
Roll it up, roll it up
Put it in a pan
And toss it in the oven, as fast as you can!

Falkner wanted to throw his whole freakin' dissertation in the oven. But he kept at it, writing about the first, much different version that was published in the late seventeenth century.

*Pat a cake, pat a cake Bakers man, so I will master
as I can, and prick it, and prick it, and prick it, and
prick it, and prick it, and throw't into the Oven.*

It didn't even rhyme.

Pat a cake, pattycake, paddycake. Who cared? Falkner had
had enough. He was sick of his thesis, sick of having it hanging
over his head, sick of the whole damned thing. Why was he
putting himself through this agony? The thought of teaching at
the end of the academic rainbow held less and less allure.

If only Aunt Ellinore would just die, he wouldn't have to
worry about finishing the stupid thesis. When he inherited all that
Duchamps money, he wouldn't have to worry about his future.
He'd be on easy street.

For distraction Falkner began surfing the Web. He entered
Piper Donovan's name to see what came up. The first entry was
something on IMDb.com. Falkner clicked and found out that
Piper was an actress. He read about the television parts she'd
played. He pored over her professional head shots—some happy,
some serious, some playful, some alluring. She was so much sexier
with her blond hair falling down around her shoulders. Why did
she always wear it up in that ponytail? If she was an actress, what
was she doing at Boulangerie Bertrand?

Though he was bored by his thesis, Falkner was more
intrigued than ever by Piper. He decided to take a walk over to
the bakery.

He was very disappointed when Piper wasn't there.

CHAPTER

39

THE TRAFFIC WAS HORRENDOUS!

Piper repeatedly looked at her watch, her stomach tensing. At one point the driver stopped to pick up more passengers. They all jammed together in the backseat of the old sedan. Piper felt better that she wasn't alone with the man in the green T-shirt anymore. Surely there was safety in numbers.

The car seemed to catch every light. Between blocks the traffic inched along. Warm, sticky air blew through the window as Piper peered out, watching men and women dressed in emerald strolling the streets, giving out flowers, beads, and kisses. As she got closer to her destination, she could hear the music of marching bands.

The driver turned around and looked at her. "I 'spect this is as close as I kin get you to Felicity and Magazine," he said. "It's about three blocks over."

"Okay. I'll get out here," said Piper. She took a twenty-dollar bill and handed it to him. "Thanks very much."

The driver appreciatively took the cash. "Thank you kindly, miss. Luck o' the Irish to you!"

PIPER RAN THE THREE BLOCKS, noticing the bright fluorescent-colored signs with arrows directing her to the location. She was overheated and out of breath when she finally reached it. She quickly found the production assistant. She handed in her passport and SAG card and filled out her paperwork. She was shown to her trailer, and then she was escorted to the wardrobe mistress and the makeup artist. At last the PA led her to an assistant director, who went over her blocking with her.

"The parade is already in full swing. You and Channing notice each other just as you are about to get onto one of the floats. You look each other up and down. You say your lines, Channing says his. Yada, yada, yada. On 'I'm Amy' you climb onto the float. He calls back to you, 'You look like a Leigh Ann to me.' You shoot the puzzled expression, and you throw him a set of beads."

"Got it," said Piper.

"Great. We'll get this going ASAP and then send you on your way until tomorrow when you do the tomb scene."

EVERYTHING HAPPENED SO QUICKLY. CHANNING Tatum came over and introduced himself. He was exactly what you'd want him to be. Charming and polite, he asked Piper about herself and even showed her a picture of his new baby on his iPhone. At one point Piper felt herself looking around wondering if this was really her life. Moments like this one made all the dry months and countless rejections worth it. She knew that it would be hard to find a girl who wouldn't kill to trade places with her right now.

The director appeared and walked Piper through her blocking for a second time. Piper listened closely so she would execute each movement exactly as instructed. The last thing she wanted was to hold up production because she hadn't been paying attention. As soon as the director walked away, a makeup woman appeared for some touch-ups.

Piper couldn't believe this was actually happening.

She took a deep breath. While she was eager to do good work and give the director what he wanted, she also knew she had to appreciate this moment as it was happening. She had wanted this. She had trained for this. She'd endured hundreds of rejections, but Piper knew that a moment like this was the payoff. She was here in costume, on a spectacular set, with a woman powdering her nose, a man making sure she was perfectly lit, and a scene partner who happened to be one of the biggest stars in the world.

This was the kind of thing that could keep her going for years.

THOUGH PIPER FELT CONFIDENT THAT her delivery had been spot-on each time, it took six takes before the director was satisfied he had what he needed. After they shot the master, they got Channing's close-ups and then hers.

When the director finally called that they were moving on, Channing said good-bye to Piper before being whisked away. Piper went back to her trailer, hung up her costume, and checked with the PA, who assured her that she was free to go for the day.

She decided to go and enjoy the parade.

Magazine Street was a sea of green. Piper reveled in the pleasure and satisfaction of having finished the scene in her first feature film as she made her way through the crowds and watched the floats decorated by New Orleans marching clubs. The float riders threw carrots, potatoes, moon pies, and beads to the onlookers gathered on the sidewalk. Pets joined in the festivities as well, sporting leprechaun attire and green-tinted fur.

Under a bright sun and a clear blue sky, families and friends were gathered for the opportunity to celebrate one of the biggest street parties of the year. Some set up ladders along the parade route, climbing atop for the best views. Others scaled trees and found perches among the branches.

"Hey, mister, throw me something!" yelled a man next to Piper.

Waving hands rose into the air as a head of cabbage came hurtling from the float. Everyone in the crowd lunged for it. The person who snagged it was roundly congratulated for the catch.

"What's with the cabbage?" Piper asked the man standing next to her.

"They aren't supposed to throw them, just hand them out.

Somebody could get hurt by one of those things." The man shrugged. "But the tradition is to cook them for dinner on St. Patrick's Day night."

Piper followed along the sidewalk, stopping to listen to the bagpipe players. She thought of her father. He loved the bagpipes. Piper wished he could see this parade. It was very different but perhaps more enjoyable than the ones in New York City he had taken her to as she grew up.

As she turned to continue up the street, Piper bumped into a puff-chested man with a florid face. He was dressed in a black suit and a green top hat. He held a long staff bedecked with giant clusters of green-and-white paper flowers at the top.

"Would you like a flower?" he asked.

"Sure. Thanks," said Piper as she selected one, pulling it out by the stem.

She was completely caught off guard when the man leaned forward and kissed her firmly on the mouth.

Startled and feeling threatened, Piper pushed the man away with a hard shove.

"Easy, *cher,*" said the beefy man. "It's a kissing cane, sweetheart. *You* get a flower. *I* get a kiss." The man chuckled as he walked away in search of his next prey.

Piper found herself angry. "Ugh, *seriously,*" she muttered.

But as she traveled farther down the sidewalk, she was aware that her extreme irritability was unreasonable. Normally she would have laughed and taken a stolen kiss in stride.

Why was she so uptight?

CHAPTER

40

Ellinore walked up and down the aisles of her shop, looking for her tricky-tray raffle donation. She tried to imagine what would be most attractive to the people attending the fund-raiser. She had a feeling that ornately fashioned sterling candlesticks wouldn't be the best for the crowd that would gather Monday evening at the Gris-Gris Bar. Young people today seemed to choose things with cleaner, simpler lines, and they certainly didn't want to polish silver. Many were much more likely to want something from Pottery Barn than from Duchamps Antiques and Illuminations.

Except for Sabrina. She was different. The young woman appreciated the beauty and workmanship of old things. Ellinore smiled when she thought of her, recalling the look of sheer delight on Sabrina's face when told that the chandelier she loved so much was to be her wedding gift.

Having Sabrina working alongside her for the past several years had given Ellinore much pleasure. Sabrina was a quick study and eager to learn about the world of antiques. Their trips together to auctions and estate sales had become joyful adventures as they hunted for treasures. Having Sabrina in the shop made the hours fly.

Ellinore knew that Sabrina in some sense was a substitute for her own daughter, the little girl who had passed away such a long time ago. While no one could ever really take Ginnie's place, there was nothing wrong with loving someone else. Human beings were meant to love, and life was empty without that. Ellinore was so grateful to be able to shower her affection on Sabrina.

She felt the ache of arthritis in her hands as she picked up a sleek crystal decanter. Ellinore considered it for her auction donation as the bell tinkled over the front door. She turned to see her nephew as he entered the shop.

"Hello, Auntie," said Falkner, thrusting a bakery box at Ellinore. "I was just at Boulangerie Bertrand, and I thought of you."

"How sweet of you, Falkner. What is it?"

"Open it up and see." He grinned, the dimples in his cheeks deepening.

Putting the box down on the mahogany sideboard, Ellinore pulled at the string and opened it.

"Voodoo-doll cookies?" she asked, smiling. "What fun! Thank you, Falkner." She held out the box. "Want one?"

"No thanks, Auntie. They're all just for you." Falkner looked around the shop but saw no customers. "Business all right?" he asked, his brow knit in concern.

"Not bad," said Ellinore. "We were quite busy this morning. It's only been slow the last hour or so."

"That's good," he said. "You deserve to be successful. You work so hard."

Watching Falkner seemingly casually peruse the merchandise, Ellinore wondered how often he tried to estimate what kind of income she earned. She'd bet it was very often. Just as she'd bet he thought all the time about inheriting her house in the Garden District. Ellinore had heard through a friend of hers that Falkner had asked a local real-estate agent to give him a ballpark estimate for the place.

"What can I bring tomorrow night?" Falkner asked as he picked up a heavy brass candlestick.

"Just yourself," said Ellinore. "You've already brought these cookies. We can have them for dessert."

"I'll look forward to it, then, Auntie." Falkner put down the candlestick. He leaned forward and kissed Ellinore on the cheek. "Is Nettie cooking?"

"No, Nettie is off on Sundays, remember? I'll be cooking myself. Pompano en papillote."

"Can't wait, Auntie," said Falkner. "You're such a good cook. See you then."

Ellinore watched with discomfort as her nephew sauntered away. Though he was related through marriage, she'd never held any affection for him, even when he was a child. There was something grasping and utterly self-absorbed about him. She still remembered how, when Ginnie was so sick, he'd never once come to visit his only cousin. Ellinore had never forgiven him for that. But boy, in recent years Falkner made it a point to stop by and visit his aging aunt and frequently wangle dinner invitations. Ellinore had no illusions about the reason.

Falkner was in for a rude awakening. Ellinore could only imagine how he would rage at the reading of her new will.

Not that she had anywhere near as much as Falkner probably thought she did. But what Ellinore did have left—the house in the Garden District and the contents of her antique shop—was not going to Falkner Duchamps.

CHAPTER

41

*I*t was time to implement step two. The next victim had been determined long ago.

It was going to be easy enough to pick up the weapon right on site, but highlighting the hoodoo connection took more planning. Invoking Damballah, the sky god, associated with creation, seemed to make sense. Damballah was represented by the serpent. His color was white. His offerings were very simple: an egg on a mound of flour or salt satisfied Damballah just fine.

Damballah was the protector of the handicapped, albinos, and young children, so it would make sense for him to be lingering near the fund-raiser for a handicapped child at the Gris-Gris Bar. Yet it was taboo to feed Damballah tobacco or alcohol in any form, so the killing couldn't take place at the bar with its drunken, smoking *patrons. It had to be done somewhere clean and white. That could be arranged.*

Damballah's corresponding figure in Catholicism was St. Patrick, the man who drove the snakes out of Ireland. How appropriate. The next hoodoo murder would take place on St. Patrick's Day.

SUNDAY
MARCH 16

CHAPTER

42

PIPER'S EYES WIDENED as she arrived at the soundstage. A deteriorating brick-and-concrete society tomb from Lafayette Cemetery No. 1 had been expertly replicated. The imposing, multilayered wall contained several burial vaults, similar to a mausoleum. Piper had read that in real life most of those buried in a society tomb were connected in some way. Lafayette Cemetery No. 1 had society tombs for volunteer firemen, orphans, members of the YMCA, and residents of the New Orleans Home for Incurables.

In *Named,* the twisted killer renamed women before murdering them and depositing them in the same tomb. It was a society that Piper never imagined she would join.

After the AD got Piper settled in her trailer, she reported to the wardrobe mistress, who gave her the same short black skirt and tight-fitting green-sequined top she'd worn in the parade scene the day before. Next Piper went to a small room at the rear of the soundstage and sat while the makeup artist applied cosmetics. Piper watched in the mirror as fake blood was dabbed at her temple and matted into her blond hair.

"Don't forget these. They're Channing's calling card."

Piper looked up and saw the reflection of the wardrobe woman behind her. She was carrying strings of green plastic beads, which she wrapped around Piper's neck.

"Nice," said Piper, managing a smile as she viewed her transformation in the mirror. "My boyfriend will love it."

When the director came over to greet her with a kiss on the cheek, Piper's heart rate increased as he began to describe what he needed from her.

"The killer thinks he's murdered you. But you're not dead— you're still alive when the killer shoves you into the tomb. You're only unconscious. You come to after he's closed your body inside."

Piper tried to nod calmly but unwillingly felt herself gulp.

"So you start out, eyes closed," continued the director. "When you open your eyes, you blink, first not comprehending where you are. Slowly it dawns on you: You're trapped. You grasp at the walls, pushing against them, struggling to get out. You scratch, you claw, you use your legs, kicking as much as you can in the confined space. Eventually, though, you realize you have to give up. Any questions, Piper?"

"No," said Piper. "I think I've got it."

"All right, then. Let's get you in there."

As the stagehands slowly slid her body into the tomb, Piper could feel her pulse pounding. She felt the heat rise in her face, and she worried about the perspiration that was beading on her forehead. It took all the control she had to stay still.

She had thought there was going to be at least some light. Instead she lay in darkness! A special camera lens, designed to record with infrared light, had been inserted into the wall of the tomb.

At the director's command, Piper closed her eyes, keeping her face expressionless, her jaw slack. She waited, trying to focus, knowing that the camera was rolling. Slowly, groggily, she opened her eyes, closed them, and then opened them again. She rolled her head from side to side.

Piper pushed her arms out tentatively, feeling for her boundaries. Her hands came into contact with the walls of the tomb. Amy, her character, still didn't know where she was. She pushed harder against the unyielding surface.

Her breath became more labored, coming in short, shallow puffs. Her fingers tensed, clawlike, as she scratched at the top of the tomb above her. She tried to kick her way out, but her legs were constricted in the tight space.

The feeling of being restrained, of not being able to move, triggered the flashback. Piper's mind raced. She was suddenly back on the hotel-room floor in Florida, with paralyzing poison coursing through her body, her head aching, perspiring profusely.

Trapped.

It became increasingly difficult to catch her breath. She struggled to get ahold of herself, to focus on where she really was. It was all make-believe. She was just acting.

As her face went numb, Piper emitted a long, piercing scream.

CHAPTER

43

THOUGH IT WASN'T the closest church to his home, Wuzzy liked attending Mass at Our Lady of Guadalupe. The church was plainer, smaller, and not as overwhelming as the cathedral. He took an odd comfort in knowing that it was the oldest surviving church building in New Orleans, originally serving as a mortuary chapel for victims of the city's yellow-fever epidemics. It reminded Wuzzy that every generation suffered.

He and Connor were ensconced in a pew near the rear of the church. After the opening hymn, the child sat on Wuzzy's lap, rocking with pleasure when the psalm was sung. But as they stood for the Gospel, Connor began to fidget in his father's arms.

When you lived in New Orleans, it was impossible not to

know when it was Lent. Mardi Gras, less than two weeks earlier, took care of that. The Gospel was about the Transfiguration, when God speaks from a bright cloud about Jesus: "This is my beloved son, with whom I am well pleased."

Wuzzy pulled his own son tighter to his broad chest, kissing the top of the boy's head. His gaze wandered to the stained-glass window depicting the angel appearing to the Blessed Virgin and announcing that she had been chosen to be the mother of God. Poor Mary, she couldn't have known the heartache and anguish she was to face. How painful it was to see your child struggle and suffer.

As the gifts were brought to the altar, Connor began to cry. Wuzzy knew there was no use trying to soothe his son. Connor's behavior wasn't going to improve. The three-year-old had had enough. Wuzzy scooped up the child and left the pew.

"You're getting heavier and heavier, kiddo," Wuzzy whispered, supporting Connor's bobbing head as they walked toward the door.

Outside, the morning air was already warm and sticky. The change in environment quieted Connor. Hoisting the boy higher on his hip, Wuzzy walked around the corner and stood beside the iron fence. Through the bars he gazed at the giant statue of St. Jude. Wuzzy thought the bearded patron saint of hopeless causes had a benevolent expression on his face.

"I've given up trying to figure out why this has happened to Connor and to me," he said softly. "And I'm realistic enough to know that some miracle isn't going to happen and make him all right. But I'd really appreciate it if you could use your influence with God and give me the strength to be the best father for Connor. I could use some help, St. Jude."

A long strand of drool dripped from Connor's mouth onto Wuzzy's loud, flower-printed sport shirt. Wuzzy knew the truth. God helped those who helped themselves.

CHAPTER

44

HER EARS WERE ringing from the reverberations of her terrified scream against the tomb walls. Piper was panting, struggling to get hold of herself. She clenched her hands into fists, trying to bring herself back into the moment. She strained to shift her mind to the present. She was only playing a part. Her poisoning in Sarasota was in the past. She had survived.

Piper could feel her body being moved. The stagehands were sliding her out of the tomb. Why weren't they moving faster? She ached to be free again.

When she finally got out, she breathed a deep sigh, releasing a bit of the tension that coursed through her system. The director was smiling broadly as he waited for her at the side of the tomb.

"Darling, that was great!" he said. "Absolutely terrific. There was nothing I'd have you do differently. You were so realistic. I can't believe we got that in one take."

"Thank you," Piper said softly.

She was weak with relief. The thought of having to do it again sickened her. She knew she couldn't go in there and do it another time.

"The scream was great," the director continued. "I'd have thought it would have been too much, but it was bloodcurdling. Just chilling, as if you really felt buried alive."

Piper nodded. "I did."

The director studied her flushed face. "Are you all right, Piper?"

"Mm-hmm. I think I need to sit for a little while."

"Of course. Take all the time you need," said the director. "You're done here for the day."

Piper slowly unwound the string of beads from around her neck, relieved at the director's praise but too unhinged to enjoy it.

CHAPTER

45

ARON WAS BENT over at his kitchen table, concentrating intensely on gluing the small pieces of the banister lining the deck of the model paddleboat. There were over a hundred tiny posts waiting to be attached, and it was a challenge getting intricate work done with his chubby fingers. But Aaron didn't mind. He relished concentrating on the task. It took his mind off his worries. Working on his models on Sundays soothed him more than going to church.

After the tension of the last few days and girding himself for the week to come, Aaron needed something to keep himself calm.

His hobby had started at the same time he began in radio. He'd gotten a job at a station on Cape Cod, not knowing a soul when he arrived. One weekend, without anything else to do, he took a whale-watching cruise. After the boat ride, he stopped at the small gift shop by the pier and purchased a kit for making a replica of an old multimasted whaling schooner. By the time he left for his next job, he still hadn't made many friends, but he had four more ship models packed carefully into cartons to move with him.

New London was twenty-five markets higher than Cape Cod on the Arbitron radio rankings and meant significant career advancement. It was also home to the United States Coast Guard Academy. Aaron became fascinated with the USCGC *Eagle,* the only active-duty tall ship, used as a training vessel for the cadets. Soon a miniature of the majestic craft stood in the middle of the fireplace mantel in the small saltbox-style house Aaron had rented. The navy's primary submarine base was also in New London and nearby Groton. So Aaron got to work on building submarine replicas as well.

It had continued like that. In Poughkeepsie, Aaron learned about the development of steam navigation on the Hudson River, the cradle of American steamboating. He'd had time to construct miniatures of the *Clermont,* the *Mary Powell,* and the *Car of Neptune* before moving on to the next-larger market. Those two years in Pensacola added battleships, aircraft carriers, and destroyers.

And on it went. By the time he arrived in New Orleans, Aaron's boats made up the bulk of his possessions. He had shelves built along the walls of his French Quarter apartment to display his treasured babies, the prized outlet for his time and loving attention.

As he put down the tube of glue, Aaron sat back and looked at the collection on the wall. There was barely a place for him to put the model of the *Natchez* when he finished with it. Maybe it was time to find another interest.

Hoodoo might be it. The more he learned about the practice, the more fascinated he became.

At the very least, Aaron didn't plan on moving to another market to find a new type of seagoing vessel to build. New Orleans was number 47 in the ratings, by far the largest market he had ever been in. He'd worked his tail off to get there. He felt satisfied in this city he loved and the place he occupied in it. He didn't want to move upward anymore, and Aaron was determined not to move down.

CHAPTER

46

EVERY SUNDAY, ELLINORE Duchamps attended Mass at the cathedral before going to her antique shop for the afternoon. Cecil waited in the pink azalea bushes until he saw her drive out of sight. He stood, brushed at his white chinos, and picked up his bag of tricks before climbing the steps to the back door.

Nettie was waiting for him, opening the door quickly and whisking him inside. She was dressed in a long, flowing white skirt and blouse. A white turban was wrapped around her head. Her feet were bare.

"Brother," she said, kissing him on the cheek.

Nettie led the way down the old wooden steps to the basement. Together they lit the two dozen candles she had arranged around a clearing at the back of the room. Then Nettie took her place in the middle of the space while Cecil took a seat on a small bench to the side. When his sister gave the signal, Cecil began patting his bongo drum.

The rhythm was slow at first. Nettie knelt down and reached into a bowl on the floor, taking pinches of flour from it. She drizzled the white powder on the dark cement, forming a cross. As she drew the lines, she chanted.

Cecil increased the tempo and began rocking to the rhythm. He joined Nettie's chanting. Their voices grew louder as they called on the spirits who linked the mortal and the immortal worlds.

Nettie rose from her knees and started to shake her *shekere,* the handmade rattle Cecil had fashioned from a hollow gourd he covered with a net of seeds, beads, and shells. Cecil banged the bongo harder and faster as Nettie began to move her body, undulating her shoulders and hips. Soon she was dancing and whirling, her long skirt billowing out around her.

Cecil got off his bench and joined his sister, dancing and praying to reaffirm the same moral principles. Reaching into his bag of tricks, Cecil felt for the leather cat-o'-nine-tails. Pulling it out, he snapped the floor with it. An angry popping sound reverberated in the dark cellar air as he tried to summon the spirits.

But he was disappointed. Cecil didn't feel the spirit mount him. Why wasn't the loa visiting him?

After they were through, Nettie collapsed while Cecil took a cigar from his bag and lit up.

"I wish you wouldn't, Cecil," she whispered, her chest heaving as she tried to catch her breath. "It's so hard to get rid of the smell. We'll give ourselves away to Miss Ellinore."

"Maybe we should invite her to join us some Sunday," Cecil said with a laugh as he blew a smoke ring into the air. "She might like it. The old girl could afford to miss a Mass."

He and Nettie had been raised Catholics, but now that they both practiced voodoo, he saw how many similarities there were between the two religions. Both believed in a supreme being. Both believed in an afterlife. Both believed that invisible demons existed. Voodoo loa were like the Christian saints who had lived exceptional lives and possessed special attributes. Followers of voodoo believed that each person had a master of the head, which corresponded to a Christian's patron saint.

"That's not funny, Cecil. You know that Miss Ellinore wouldn't approve. With all the talk about the Hoodoo Killer on Royal Street, Miss Ellinore would likely lose her mind if she knew what we do down here."

"Makes no difference to me if she approves or not," said Cecil, putting out the cigar. "But I don't want to get you in no trouble, Nettie."

CHAPTER

47

O N THE TAXI ride back to the French Quarter, Piper's cell phone rang. It was Marguerite.

"I was wondering if you might like to have something to eat with me at Napoleon House."

"Yeah, that sounds great," said Piper, not wanting to be alone. After shooting the tomb scene, she needed to be in the land of the living again.

Piper had read about Napoleon House online. The place was listed as the former residence of a mayor of New Orleans who had offered his home to Napoleon Bonaparte as a refuge during his island exile. Napoleon died before sympathetic New Orleanians could rescue him, but now the three-story example of Creole architecture was registered as a National Historic Landmark and housed a bar and restaurant. It was on Chartres, just a block over from Royal.

When she arrived, Piper spotted Marguerite waiting for her out front. The line moved quickly, and the two of them entered the building and proceeded into a dimly lit, weathered-looking bar area. Old prints, proclamations, and newspaper articles were framed and hung on the mottled walls. Smiling, chattering patrons ate and drank at the banged-up tables. Classical music played on the sound system.

They followed the hostess through the bar area into an adjoining room that, like the rest of the place, also had an overall cocoonlike feeling of benign neglect. An old black fan whirred from the chipped, brown-painted ceiling. A portrait of Napoleon and other varied faded pictures decorated the walls. The terrazzo floor was scuffed. Piper and Marguerite were escorted to a small round table placed beside French doors that opened directly out to the sidewalk.

They both ordered red beans and rice with sausage and a side salad.

"And to drink?" asked the old waiter.

"Um, I'm not sure," said Piper, glancing at Marguerite. She was in New Orleans. Ordering a club soda seemed boring and unadventurous. "What do you suggest?"

The waiter shrugged. "The house specialty is the Pimm's Cup."

"Which is what, exactly?" asked Piper.

"A gin-based British liqueur, lemonade, and a splash of lemon-lime soda," answered the waiter. "It's very refreshing."

"Okay. I'll have that."

"Make that two," said Marguerite.

While they sipped their drinks, Piper told Marguerite about the morning filming, confiding how terrified she'd been when trapped inside the fake crypt.

"I had an experience recently that I'd really rather not talk about," said Piper. "But being unable to move just brought back the terror of the whole thing." She shook her head to clear it. "This is such a fantastic, magical place, though. I don't want to focus on the negative while I'm here. I really want to enjoy New Orleans."

"I'm so sorry for your struggle, Piper, but I'm glad you're enjoying our city," said Marguerite, smiling. "I love it, too."

"Were you born here?" asked Piper.

"Yes. I grew up in a little shotgun house, eating creole food and listening to jazz. When I was young, I took it all for granted. It's only now that I truly appreciate how special this town is. I'd never want to live anyplace else."

"I can sure see why," said Piper, taking a sip of her Pimm's Cup.

The waiter brought the plates to the table. As Piper picked up her fork, her mouth turned down at the corners.

"Is something wrong?" asked Marguerite with concern etched on her face. "Isn't the food what you expected?"

"Oh, no. It's not that," said Piper. "I was just thinking about those men in the store yesterday morning. They gave me the feeling you might be changing locations, leaving New Orleans."

Marguerite cocked her head. "What men?"

"The three guys who came in and talked with Bertrand. They walked around the shop measuring and taking pictures. One of them was asking the customers questions."

"What kinds of questions?" asked Marguerite.

"Like, if they would come to the bakery if it were someplace else."

"But where would it be?" asked Marguerite.

Piper shrugged. "I have no idea. The man didn't name a place. It was just a general question. Anyway, sorry, it's really none of my business."

"I appreciate your concern, Piper," said Marguerite as she slid some rice onto her fork. "That's really very sweet of you. But you have nothing to worry about. We often have people coming in to take a peek at how we do things. Maybe they have a business of their own and were looking for ideas. I don't know what those men were doing in the bakery, but Boulangerie Bertrand is staying in New Orleans, right where it belongs."

CHAPTER

48

AFTER LUNCH WITH Marguerite, Piper considered going to the bakery, but all she really wanted was to go upstairs to her little apartment and relax. Bertrand had said that he didn't expect her to work on Sundays, but Piper had had every intention of spending whatever was left of her day helping him out. That was before. Now she decided to take Bertrand up on his offer.

She let herself through the black iron gate, locked it, and slowly climbed the stairs. Once in the apartment—and carefully locking that door, too—Piper kicked off her shoes, went to the kitchen, and poured herself a glass of orange juice. She gulped it down and poured herself another, which she took with her to the bedroom. Sitting on the bed, she called Jack. Piper could hear the television set blaring in the background when he answered.

"What are you doing?" she asked.

"Watching the basketball game."

"I forgot," said Piper. "March Madness. Let me tell you, the craziness is alive and well here in New Orleans."

"I don't know why, Pipe. LSU doesn't look good for the Final Four."

"That's not the madness I meant. It's me, Jack. I feel like I'm losing it."

Piper heard the background noise cease as Jack immediately turned down the sound on his television.

"What's wrong?" he asked.

She told him about shooting the scene in the tomb. "It was horrible, Jack," she said as she wrapped up her story. "It brought back all those awful feelings. I felt totally paralyzed and scared out of my mind."

"And what did the director say?" asked Jack.

Piper managed a little laugh. "Oh, he was thrilled. He thought it was perfect, that I was flawless. I wonder what he'd say if he knew I wasn't acting. He'd probably be even more thrilled. Nothing beats authenticity. I was basically reliving something that had pretty much already happened to me. Method acting at its finest."

"A flashback," said Jack. "I'm no doctor, Pipe. But I do know that flashbacks are symptoms of PTSD."

"Post-traumatic stress disorder? Me? Please, Jack. No way."

"Why should *you* be immune? You went through a dangerous, life-threatening event, Piper."

"It's not like I got bombed in Afghanistan or something."

"You don't have to be a soldier to suffer from PTSD," he answered. "When we're in danger, it's only natural to feel afraid.

That fear triggers many split-second responses in the body to defend itself. The 'fight-or-flight' response." Jack slowed his speech a little. "But in PTSD the reaction is changed. With PTSD you can feel stressed or frightened even when you aren't in actual danger anymore."

Piper took a sip of juice and considered his words. Though she didn't like to hear it, Jack was making sense.

"Okay. Let's just say you're right," she said. "What do I do about it?"

"I don't really know enough about it, Pipe, but for starters I'd imagine that professional help would be a good idea," Jack said quietly.

"I want to go home, Jack."

"Come home, then," he urged. "Come home, Piper."

"I can't, Jack. I can't run out on Bertrand and Marguerite. I'm committed, and I want to see it through."

"All right." He sighed. "I suppose waiting another week or two to see a doctor won't be the end of the world. But you have to promise me that you'll call if something like this happens again, Pipe. Call me if anything at all bothers you."

"Don't worry. I will," answered Piper. "I feel like I need to get this under control or else I won't even be able to act anymore. It really scared me, Jack."

CHAPTER

49

Jack pumped the sound back up on the television, but he couldn't focus on the game. After fifteen minutes of turning the conversation with Piper over in his mind, he reached for his phone. He called the FBI operator and asked to be connected to Nick Kilcannon at home.

"Hey, Jack," said the bureau psychologist when the connection was made. "What's up?"

"Sorry to bother you at home on a Sunday, Nick. You're in the middle of watching the game, right?"

"As a matter of fact, I'm not. I guess I'm one of the few men in America who couldn't care less."

"The only one I know." Jack chuckled. "But that's good for me. I have a personal situation I was hoping I could run by you. It's my girlfriend. I'm worried about her."

"Sure. Go ahead, shoot."

Jack's tone turned serious as he explained the situation: Piper, the paralyzing puffer-fish poisoning in Sarasota the month before, administered by a killer she'd uncovered, how deathly ill Piper had been, and the flashback she'd experienced this morning. The psychologist listened in silence while Jack told the story.

"So I was thinking Piper might be dealing with PTSD," Jack finished. "What do you think?"

"It sounds like she's had the first 'reexperiencing' symptom," said Nick. "Have there been any avoidance symptoms?"

"Avoidance symptoms?" asked Jack, grabbing a pencil and pad. "What do you mean?"

"Has she wanted to stay away from places or things that remind her of what happened to her?"

As he ran the fingers of his free hand through his dark hair, Jack thought about it. "Well, she's refused to eat seafood since it happened, but I can't think of anything else."

"Depression, worry, guilt?" asked Nick. "Has she mentioned that she feels emotionally numb?"

"No on the numbness—or at least she hasn't said anything about that to me. But I'd say she's definitely worried," answered Jack. "And guilt? I don't think so. She hasn't seemed really depressed either. Tired sometimes, and a little listless, which would make sense after how sick she was, but not really depressed."

"Okay. Has she lost interest in activities that she previously enjoyed?"

Jack considered before answering. "Not that I've noticed."

"And you tell me she has no trouble remembering what happened to her when she was poisoned?"

"No," said Jack. "I'd say she remembers it all too well."

"How about hyperarousal? Have you noticed her being easily startled? Does she seem tense or on edge?"

"A little bit maybe."

"What about sleep? Is she having problems sleeping?"

"Yeah," said Jack "She's complained of not being able to fall asleep and waking up a lot during the night when she does."

"Any angry outbursts?"

"None that I've seen."

"Watch for those, Jack. Watch for all the things we've just talked about. But I think it may be a little early to be diagnosing PTSD. Piper would have to have at least three of the avoidance symptoms and two of the hyperarousal symptoms for at least a month. It doesn't sound like she's there yet. With luck, she may never be."

"So that's all there is to do at this point?" asked Jack. "Keep an eye on her? That's hard, since she's in New Orleans. But I'll try my best to stay on top of how she's doing."

"I have no doubt about that, Jack. And I'll give you the name of a psychologist for Piper to see if she wants to talk to somebody when she comes back north. In the meantime don't hesitate to give me a call if you need to."

"Thanks, Nick, but I hope I've just overreacted."

"Better safe than sorry, buddy. Besides, some people with PTSD don't show any symptoms for weeks or months. It could be a while before you know with a fair amount of certainty that Piper is out of the woods."

CHAPTER

50

CLOSING HER ANTIQUE shop precisely at five o'clock, Ellinore stopped to buy pompano fillets, crabmeat, mushrooms, and green onions before going home. Falkner was coming for dinner. She wanted to feed him well before she broke the news to him.

She didn't have to tell him, of course. He would learn the upsetting truth when she died. But somehow it didn't seem right to let her nephew go on thinking that he was going to be the heir to whatever she had left when she departed this world.

The Duchamps fortune was long gone, and Ellinore had supported herself for years now. Falkner could do the same. Still, she did feel a tad guilty that she wasn't leaving him the house that had been built by the Duchamps family. But she'd been able to hold on to it only because she'd worked so hard. It was *hers* now, and she could do with it as she pleased. Ellinore wanted Sabrina to have it, almost as much as she would have wanted Ginnie to have the place if she'd lived.

Ellinore loved Sabrina like a daughter. She did not love Falkner. Nor had Falkner shown any real love for her. More important, he hadn't shown any concern or compassion for Ginnie.

As she chopped the mushrooms and green onions and browned them in butter, Ellinore wondered how Falkner would take it. She doubted he would react with good grace. She hoped he wouldn't lose his temper or get aggressive.

She mixed two tablespoons of flour into the vegetables, then added stock and seasoning and set it all to boil for a few minutes. Next came the white wine. Ellinore had to go downstairs to the basement to get a bottle.

The moment she opened the cellar door, Ellinore detected it. As she started down the basement steps, the unmistakable cigar smell grew stronger.

What was Nettie doing down here?

Ellinore started searching for clues. At first everything looked normal. Nettie's little room at the north end of the cellar was neat as usual. It gave no hint that Nettie had been staying there, though Ellinore well knew she had.

Slowly, Ellinore got down on her hands and knees, pushed back the coverlet, and looked under the bed. She reached in and felt something hard and smooth. She pulled out a black candle, then another and another. Two dozen in all.

She rose to her feet, left the sleeping area, and continued to search. It dawned on Ellinore what she was dealing with when she spotted the smudged white cross on the dark cement floor.

CHAPTER

51

I T WAS TWILIGHT as Piper walked into the Gris-Gris Bar. She went up to the counter and took a seat, grateful for the pulsating music blaring from the speakers in the corners of the room. She ordered a glass of white wine and tapped her foot as she waited for it. She was glad to be around people.

The bartender slid a stemmed glass in front of her. "There you go," he said. "Let me know how you like it. I'm trying a new brand of pinot grigio."

"Thanks," said Piper, taking a sip. "Mmm. I like that. Really light. Good choice."

"Glad you like it," said the bartender. "And I'm Wuzzy, by the way."

"Hey, Wuzzy-by-the-way. I'm Piper." She reached out, and they shook hands.

"And I'm Falkner-by-the-way."

Piper looked in the direction of the voice. Falkner Duchamps had taken his place on the bar stool next to hers. What was that old-fashioned expression her mother always used? The one about turning up like a bad penny? Falkner seemed to be everywhere. Actually, she wasn't unhappy about seeing him right now. At least Falkner was somebody she knew, even if only a little. At this point Piper welcomed a semifamiliar face.

"You get around, don't you?" she asked.

Falkner smirked. "I could say the same about you."

"If this clown bothers you, just let me know, Piper," said Wuzzy, nodding at Falkner and smiling. "I know how annoying he can be."

"Aw, Wuz, don't give Piper a bad impression of me," said Falkner. "I can do that all on my own."

When Wuzzy went to serve another customer, Falkner told Piper about the bartender's son and the fund-raiser that was being held the next night.

"I heard Bertrand and Marguerite talking about what they're donating," said Piper. "Poor little Connor and poor Wuzzy. That's a lot to handle."

"I know," said Falkner. "It's heartbreaking. But money would make things a lot easier. I have the feeling that though this may be the first fund-raiser we hold, it won't be the last. There will be a lifetime of expenses. If I were Wuzzy, I think I'd have snapped by now."

Piper thought she noticed a tear at the corner of Falkner's eye. She was touched by the empathy he was showing. Perhaps she had misjudged him. Maybe he was more than a wannabe player and ladies' man. Suddenly the idea that Falkner might have the sensitivity to explore the origins and meanings of nursery rhymes didn't seem so outlandish.

Wuzzy came back to them, holding a glass beer mug in his hand and drying it with a dish towel. "So what's new, Falkner?" he asked. "Hear anything interesting out on the street?"

"As a matter of fact, I did hear something," said Falkner. "I heard the cops think they have a solid lead in Muffuletta Mike's murder. Apparently they found a single very clear fingerprint in the blood at the sandwich shop."

The mug suddenly slipped from Wuzzy's big hand and crashed onto the floor. He stepped back quickly, trying to avoid the flying glass shards. Falkner put his hands out in front of Piper's face, shielding her from any wayward fragments.

"I don't know what's the matter with me," said Wuzzy, his face reddening. "Nerves, I guess. That's the third glass I've broken today."

MONDAY
MARCH 17
ST. PATRICK'S DAY

CHAPTER

52

*T*hough *the biggest parade had taken place on Saturday in the Garden District, the St. Patrick's Day festivities carried through to the actual feast day. Why celebrate on just one day when you could stretch the party out over a long weekend?*

It should be easy to blend in with the drunken, green-garbed revelers in the French Quarter tonight.

The first blood-drenched murder scene had gotten some people talking about a hoodoo connection, and Friday night's radio show had helped spread the word. But New Orleans wasn't really buzzing yet about Muffuletta Mike's death and its link to hoodoo. After tonight that would change. There would be no ignoring the Hoodoo Killer on the loose.

To make the hoodoo connection, the clues to Damballah, one of the most important loa, had to be there for all to see. A mound of flour crowned with an egg would be a sign of the simple offering to the spirit. White was Damballah's color, and it would be well represented at the murder scene. But to make absolutely sure there would be no doubt, Damballah's symbol, the serpent, had to be present. A snake had to be left beside the dead body.

With no desire to care for the reptile or take the chance that anyone else would see it, the visitor to the pet shop had left the actual purchase of the snake until now. A salesclerk in the pet store pointed the way to the reptile section. Glass tanks were stacked on the back wall, showcasing a wide selection of snakes.

So many different varieties, their skins in striking colors and patterns, their bodies slithering and coiling! Pythons, boas, king snakes, corn snakes, milk snakes. Striped snakes, spotted snakes, black snakes, orange snakes, green snakes. It was mesmerizing to see their undulating bodies and flicking tongues.

A salesclerk strolled over. "They're amazing, aren't they?" he asked.

The customer nodded. "Very."

"Snakes are such popular pets," the clerk continued. "They're easy to care for, they have minimal odor, and they tend to be quite docile. They're fascinating to learn about, too. I can spend hours watching them."

The customer pointed at one of the tanks. Inside, an icy gray snake with white stripes was twisted in the corner. Beady red eyes protruded from the sides of its head.

"Tell me about that one."

"That's our albino California king snake," said the salesclerk. "It's a solitary snake and shouldn't be housed with others. It usually sleeps *during the day. You'll see it move most during the night or twilight hours."*

"What does it eat?"

"It's a carnivore. Strictly a meat eater. We recommend and sell frozen mice here."

The customer browsed the adjoining tanks, looking at the other snakes before coming back to the gray one.

"We're running a sale this week," said the salesclerk. "This snake is twenty dollars less than it usually is."

"Okay," answered the customer. "I'll take it."

The clerk smiled. "Good. Is this your first snake? Or do you already have everything you need?"

"Tell me what you mean."

"Well, you need a terrarium, of course. A water dish, lighting and heating elements, a thermometer. That snake likes to burrow, so I'd recommend some aspen bedding."

The customer considered the information before agreeing to the extra purchases. It was better to seem like someone who was serious about maintaining the snake long-term. Not someone who was using it for one night only. If the details about tonight's murder were reported in the news and the clerk saw or heard about the snake at the crime scene, he might recall the customer who had bought only the snake but nothing with which to sustain it.

The salesclerk gathered the paraphernalia and the frozen mice, packed it all up, and slid a brochure about proper handling of snakes into one of the bags. The customer paid for everything with cash.

CHAPTER

53

Nettie waited until she saw Miss Ellinore back her car down the driveway. Once the car was out of sight, she emerged from behind the massive azalea bush and let herself into the house. She was putting on her apron when she heard the crunch of footsteps on the pea-gravel path.

Nettie peeked out of the kitchen window. Miss Ellinore was back and walking up to the door!

Before Nettie could turn and run down the basement steps to hide, Ellinore entered the room.

"Oh, Miss Ellinore, you scared me," said Nettie as she put her hand over her heart. She quickly thought of an explanation for her presence in the house. "I hope you don't mind if I work today instead of Wednesday. I got a doctor appointment Wednesday. I was gonna leave you a note."

"No, I don't mind, Nettie," Ellinore said coolly. "Is everything all right?"

"Yes, ma'am. Everything fine. I just has a little checkup, that's all. Did you forget something, Miss Ellinore? Is that why you came back?"

"No, Nettie. I didn't forget anything." Ellinore sighed heavily. "I guess I just wanted to catch you off your guard."

Nettie looked uncertainly at her boss. "Why'd you want to do that, Miss Ellinore?"

"I know what you've been doing, Nettie."

Casting her eyes to the floor, Nettie felt her heart beat faster. "What you mean, Miss Ellinore?"

"You know what I mean, Nettie," said Ellinore. "I'll admit I've known that you've been staying in the house, helping me even though you weren't getting paid for most of your work. I've taken advantage of your loyalty and allowed it. I liked having this place kept up the way you do. So I've been wrong, too. Wrong and selfish. I'm sorry."

Nettie looked up and met Ellinore's gaze. "That's all right, Miss Ellinore. I want to be here with you. I want to help you. I feel more at home here than I do at Rhonda's house. That husband of hers is no good, and he barely puts up with me. I'd rather be here with you."

Ellinore shook her head ruefully. "You can't," she said. "I can't have you here anymore. At all."

Nettie recoiled as if struck. "I don't understand," she stuttered.

"I can't have voodoo practiced in my house. I won't stand for it."

"But, Miss Ellinore—"

"Don't insult me by denying it, Nettie," Ellinore said firmly as she crossed her arms over her chest. "We both know very well what you've been doing in the cellar."

Nettie's eyes filled with tears. "I promise, ma'am. I won't ever do it again. Never. I give my word."

"No, Nettie. You have to leave."

"But, Miss Ellinore, I spent my life helping you and your family."

"I know you have, Nettie, but no more. Please, leave this house now and don't ever come back."

CHAPTER

54

WE NEED MORE green beignets out front," called Piper as she hurried into the kitchen. "They're selling like hotcakes." She paused and smiled. "Literally."

Bertrand pointed to a large tray of the square, holeless doughnuts on the worktable. "And I have more frying now, Piper. Don't worry. We're used to this." He reached over and put his hand on her shoulder, holding on a little too long for it to be merely a reassuring gesture.

Through the morning and into the afternoon, the customers continued to come into the bakery, buying boxes and bags of green alligator bread, leprechaun-hat cookies, shamrock-shaped coffee cakes, Irish soda bread, and hot cross buns. Piper helped out in the front of the store, filling and ringing up orders. She found herself avoiding Bertrand as much as possible.

At four o'clock Marguerite asked Piper if she would mind carrying some boxes of baked goods for that evening's fund-raiser over to the Gris-Gris Bar.

"Of course not," said Piper. "I'd be glad to."

"Great," said Marguerite. "I appreciate that, Piper. And after you drop those off, you're finished here for the day. Go upstairs, rest, and get ready for tonight. We'll see you at the fund-raiser later."

Piper didn't protest. She welcomed the chance to knock off early. The bakery wasn't a comfortable place for her anymore.

As SHE CROSSED THE STREET to the Gris-Gris Bar, Piper spotted a white van parked out front. The sign on the side announced that the van belonged to a local radio station.

Carrying the bakery boxes inside and resting them on a table, she scanned the bar. There were only a few customers at the counter, but she noticed other people busily moving around in the rest of the space. A woman was stringing green crepe paper and tiny white lights from the ceiling. One man carried electrical equipment to a spot at the side of the room, while another unwound some cables. A third man, wearing headphones, sat at a table with a microphone and a laptop computer positioned in front of him. Piper thought he looked somewhat familiar, but she was distracted by something else. A blond-haired little boy with a cherubic face lay on his stomach in a playpen in the middle of the floor. He had propped himself on his elbows while holding a dish towel in his hand and rubbing the playpen floor with it.

"Hiya, handsome," Piper cooed as she bent down to get closer. "Whatcha doing?"

"Wub-a-dub. Wub-a-dub." The child smiled, his blue eyes twinkling from behind the glasses perched on his small nose.

"You're cleaning up, huh?" asked Piper. "You're good at that."

She talked to the boy for a while longer. He talked back, but Piper could understand almost nothing of what he said. She noticed that his young body was really too large for the limited playpen space. His feet pushed against the mesh wall, while the top of his head pushed against the opposite one. But the boy seemed unconcerned and comfortable enough, while Piper supposed that his father's main concern was limiting the child from crawling away and getting hurt.

Piper knew that she wanted to have kids someday. Friends of hers had already started having babies. It awed her to see how much time infants demanded, how many details had to be attended to. And as they grew, so did the responsibilities. Once the baby started crawling, toddling, and walking, there was no end to the new things that could lead to trouble. Her friends with children hardly ever wanted to go out at night anymore. They were too tired after a day of child care and always cognizant of the fact that there would be more of the same the following day. They wanted to go to bed early because they would be getting up early and starting all over again.

Now, as she considered the child in the playpen, Piper was acutely aware that her exhausted friends were so fortunate. They had kids who were meeting all the developmental milestones.

They were sitting up and walking and talking clearly. Piper didn't even want to imagine what it would be like to have a child who didn't, couldn't, progress as he should.

"I see you've met my son."

Piper looked up to see Wuzzy towering above her. She stood to face him, noticing the lines on the bartender's forehead and around his eyes and mouth. Piper suspected that Wuzzy spent much of his time fretting about his son's problems, his face set in a worried frown.

"We've been having a nice conversation," said Piper. "He seems like such a happy little guy."

Wuzzy nodded. "Connor is a pretty cheerful kid, thank goodness. So far he doesn't show much frustration at his limitations."

They both looked on as Connor continued to move the towel in a circular motion on the playpen floor.

"Wub-a-dub. Wub-a-dub."

As Piper turned to leave the bar to go home to bathe and dress, she glanced over again at the table covered with microphones and audio equipment. A banner had been attached to the edge: NOLA RADIO 666.

Wuzzy followed her gaze. "I know," he said. "Go figure. *The Aaron Kane Show* is broadcasting live from here tonight. I couldn't believe it when Aaron came in and told me he wanted to bring attention to Connor and help raise more money for his care."

"That was very nice of him," said Piper.

"You're not kidding." Wuzzy leaned closer to Piper and lowered his voice. "I always thought Kane was sorta pompous and full of himself, if you know what I mean. But I guess he has a kind, altruistic side after all. Just goes to show you never know about people, do you?"

"No, I guess not," answered Piper. But as she regarded Aaron Kane one more time, she realized why he looked familiar to her. He was the man with the flowered kissing cane who had planted the sloppy smooch on her lips at the parade in the Garden District.

CHAPTER

55

THE FRONT DOOR was locked, and the Closed sign was hanging in the bakery window. Marguerite had gone home to shower and change before meeting up with Bertrand at the fund-raiser later. Bertrand was relieved to have some time all alone in the shop. There was a phone conversation he wanted to have while he had a little privacy.

He made the call but got voice mail.

"Hello. It is Bertrand. Give me a call. I am afraid we may have a small problem. It is not insurmountable, but I want to talk to you about one of the provisions in the contract. I will be here at the bakery for another hour or so."

Bertrand cleaned his work area, wiping down the long, wooden table and placing bowls, measuring cups, spoons, and mixing paddles in the industrial dishwasher. He didn't want to turn the machine on until just before he left for the fund-raiser. The thing made such a racket.

There would be a light repast after Muffuletta Mike's funeral tomorrow morning. Boulangerie Bertrand was supplying pastries, which were already made and packed in boxes tied with twine. Between making those along with the desserts for tonight's fund-raiser and the St. Patrick's Day goodies for the regular customers, Bertrand had kept the ovens and mixers running all day.

As he carried the pastries to the walk-in refrigerator, Bertrand thought he heard a noise. He stopped. Was someone in the corridor? Was someone in the display and sales area?

Standing still, he strained to hear. He could feel heat rise in his face, adrenaline in response to a perceived threat. But the only sound he heard was footsteps coming from the floor above.

He calculated where exactly the footsteps were falling in the upstairs apartment and decided that Piper was in the bathroom. His supposition was confirmed when he heard the sound of water beginning to flow through the old iron pipes. Piper was drawing a bath.

Did he dare?

Could he use the dumbwaiter and go up? Could he catch a glimpse of her as she bathed, unaware that he was peeking at her from around the corner? The thought of it left him terribly excited. But it was very dangerous. It was one thing to sneak up there and watch Piper in the middle of the night while she slept. It was quite another to venture into the apartment while she was wide awake.

He knew he was taking an incredible chance, yet that only made it more thrilling. Bertrand began to breathe faster and more heavily, knowing that if he was going to do it, he should get into the dumbwaiter and start up there now, while the water was still running.

He kicked off his shoes, ripped away his baker's jacket, and headed for the corridor. He silently opened the door to the dumbwaiter and began to climb inside. He faced into the dark compartment, his back to the hallway. He didn't sense the stealthy movement behind him or feel anything until the steel point of the flower nail jammed with deadly force into the side of his neck.

CHAPTER

56

THE TUB WAS filling. Piper lifted her foot, stuck her toe over the edge, and tested the water. Not hot enough. She turned the handle and adjusted the temperature upward.

As she twisted her blond hair into a bun and fastened it to the back of her head, Piper thought she heard a heavy thud come from below. She imagined that a giant bag of flour or sugar could have fallen onto the floor in the bakery kitchen. She paid little attention.

Sinking gratefully into the soothing bath, she let out a long, deep sigh. She wished she could stay right here. A leisurely soak followed by ordering in some dinner and an evening watching TV would suit her just fine. But she had committed to attending the fund-raiser, and she wanted to support Wuzzy and Connor. She didn't have to stay late, but she did have to go.

She leaned her head against the back of the tub and closed her eyes.

PIPER REALIZED SHE HAD DOZED off. The water in the tub was decidedly cooler, and ridges had developed on the skin of her fingers and toes. She rose from the bath and dried herself off.

What to wear?

As she perused the garments hanging in the closet, she supposed she should choose something in honor of St. Patrick's Day. But between the parade attire she'd watched revelers wearing, the film shoots where she'd worn the emerald-colored sequined number, and all the tinted bakery goods she'd been making, wrapping, and selling over the past few days, Piper was over green. She picked out a fresh white T-shirt and her favorite jeans and called it a day, knowing that there was no dress code at the Gris-Gris Bar.

When she arrived, the place was packed. Piper was amazed at how many people were familiar to her now after just her few days in New Orleans. It pleased her to see Sabrina and Leo at the bar talking to Wuzzy. Aaron Kane was at his table speaking into a microphone for his radio show. He appeared to be interviewing another man, someone Piper didn't recognize. She walked closer, listened to the ongoing radio conversation, and learned that the man was another Royal Street merchant who was supporting a neighbor and fellow businessman and his son. Aaron spotted Piper watching and nodded at her.

A jazz band played in the corner of the bar. Piper recognized one of the musicians as the seemingly angry man she had seen at Muffuletta Mike's on her first day in New Orleans and then heard talking to a cop about a hoodoo connection to Mike's murder the next day. The musician was dressed in white pants and a white shirt. He wore a porkpie hat on the back of his head and a plush toy snake, striped with yellow, green, and purple, around his neck.

He may have felt Piper watching him, because when there was a break in the music, he beckoned to her to come over.

"Anything you want to hear, miss?" he asked. The man didn't appear to recognize Piper.

She considered for a moment. "It's not very original, but how about 'When Irish Eyes Are Smiling'?"

On cue a trumpet, a saxophone, a trombone, and a bass joined the clarinet in the familiar tune, though Piper had never heard a jazz rendition of it. She and the others gathered in the bar applauded heartily when the song ended.

"That was great!" yelled Piper over the din.

The musician tipped his hat toward her. "Glad you liked it, miss."

Piper wanted to talk with the musician, but she didn't want to open with the fact that she'd seen his annoyed departure from Muffuletta Mike's or had overheard his conversation with the police officer about the murder. Those weren't exactly conversation starters. Instead she asked the next question that popped into her mind.

"Is that snake around your neck supposed to signify St. Patrick driving the snakes out of Ireland?" she asked.

"If that's what you want to believe, miss. But in my religion the spirit Damballah is St. Patrick's counterpart," the musician said proudly. "And Damballah is represented by the serpent. That's why I wear the snake, and that's why I wear white tonight. The spirit Damballah's color is white."

Before Piper could respond, someone else yelled, "Cecil! Hey, man, are we playing or not?" The trumpet player was looking at Cecil with an exasperated expression on his face.

"All right, all right," said Cecil, raising his clarinet. He looked at Piper. "I'm sorry, miss, but I have to get back to work."

TABLES HAD BEEN SET UP to display the donated prizes for the tricky tray. Fund-raiser participants purchased tickets for cash and then deposited the tickets in bowls placed in front of the prize or prizes they wanted to win.

Piper spent fifty dollars on ten raffle tickets, green and shaped like shamrocks. She scribbled her name on the back of each one. She put five of them in the bowl to win the brass candlesticks from Duchamps Antiques and Illuminations. As she deposited her remaining shamrocks for a chance to win another session with the Royal Street fortune-teller, Piper felt a hand on her arm. It belonged to Falkner Duchamps. His face dimpled as he smiled at her.

"So you want to know what the future holds, huh, Piper?"

"Doesn't everyone?"

"Well, you're talking to the guy who'll be pulling out the winners tonight," said Falkner. "I'll see what I can do."

"Now, I wouldn't want any preferential treatment," said Piper. "Aw, what fun is that?"

Piper laughed. She glanced around the room and said, "I haven't seen Bertrand and Marguerite yet tonight. Have you?"

Falkner pointed. "I saw Marguerite over there," he said. "But don't run off, Piper. Keep me company. I can make sure it's worth your while."

Piper waved as she walked away. "See you later, buddy."

MARGUERITE WAS AT THE BUFFET sampling the food from Bistro Sabrina.

"These crab cakes are delicious, and the Gulf oysters are sublime. Try some, Piper."

Piper made a little face. "No thanks, I haven't had much of an appetite for seafood in a while. I think I'll indulge my sweet tooth instead."

She selected a cookie from Boulangerie Bertrand. It was shaped like a bathtub with three men's heads peeking from the top. They'd made the nursery-rhyme cookies as a tip of the hat to Connor.

"Rub-a-dub-dub, three men in a tub," said Piper. "Bertrand and you do such a great job with these things. I gotta tell you, I'm definitely going to steal this idea and take it back north with me."

"Imitation is the sincerest form of flattery, right?" asked Marguerite. "Bertrand and I will be flattered to think our cookies are being copied."

"Where *is* Bertrand?" asked Piper, looking around again. "I haven't seen him yet."

"I was just wondering the same thing," said Marguerite, pulling her cell phone from her purse. "I went home to shower and dress. We were supposed to meet up here."

When the phone call to her husband went directly to voice mail, Marguerite looked at Piper and made a suggestion. "Let's go over to the bakery and see what's keeping him."

THE NIGHT AIR WAS BALMY as they crossed Royal Street. Piper and Marguerite jostled their way through the St. Patrick's Day celebrants. Shamrocks, green T-shirts, and leprechaun hats were the dominant apparel. Many pedestrians carried cans of beer and cocktails in plastic cups as they sang and danced, turning the road into a street party.

"And just think!" Marguerite yelled over the noise to Piper. "In another two days we'll be celebrating St. Joseph's Day!"

Approaching the bakery, they saw that the Closed sign was in the window. A single night-light dimly illuminated the display room. But, beyond that, a bright beam streamed from the kitchen out into the corridor. Neither woman could detect any movement inside.

Marguerite took out her keys and unlocked the front door, immediately disarming the alarm as they entered. She called out. "Bertrand?"

Flipping the switch for the chandeliers, Marguerite called out again as the room was immediately filled with light. "Bertrand?"

Piper followed as Marguerite led the way toward the kitchen. When she heard Marguerite's gasp, Piper was seized with fright as she forced herself to look.

Bertrand lay in the middle of the corridor floor, a puddle of blood next to his head. Piper looked on in horror as she realized that a flower needle was sticking from his neck.

"Oh, my God, Piper! Call 911!" screamed Marguerite as she collapsed onto her knees beside her husband. She reached over and touched his face, then shook him by the shoulders.

"Bertrand, Bertrand!" she yelled. "Wake up!"

Piper made the emergency call, quickly giving the information the dispatcher required. "They're on their way, Marguerite," she said, trying to keep the panic from her voice.

Marguerite put her ear to her husband's chest and then next to his mouth. "I can't hear a heartbeat!" she cried. "He's not breathing!"

"I know CPR," said Piper. "Let me try."

Even as she started chest compressions, Piper was fairly sure it was too late. The effort to make the heart pump again and get blood and oxygen to keep the brain functioning could be a precious lifesaving tool. Though CPR usually worked on TV shows, it was nowhere near as successful in real life. It was only likely to be effective if started within six minutes after the blood stopped flowing. Looking at Bertrand's open mouth and ashen face was discouraging. Piper also could see that blood wasn't seeping from his neck wound and most likely hadn't been even as Marguerite had tried calling him from the Gris-Gris Bar. Those critical six minutes had come and were probably long gone.

But she continued with the compressions until the EMTs got there.

THE POLICE ARRIVED AS THE paramedic stated the obvious: Bertrand Olivier was dead.

Piper watched as the body was examined. She hadn't noticed until now the mound of white powder that had been formed near Bertrand's feet or the egg that had been placed on top of it. In fact, there was a white dusting over almost the entire hallway. Piper looked down at her arms and legs, noting that after kneeling on the floor beside Bertrand she was covered in the white powder as well.

"Flour," remarked one of the officers.

Piper held Marguerite as she wept while the police took pictures of the body and the rest of the crime scene from every imaginable angle. When a detective asked for details of what had happened in the time leading up to the discovery of the body, Marguerite looked helplessly at Piper.

"I just can't talk—not now," she whispered.

Piper answered. "We were supposed to meet up with Bertrand at the Gris-Gris Bar across the street for the fund-raiser there tonight," she explained. "When he didn't show up, we came here to look for him. We found him on the floor."

"Was the door unlocked?" asked the detective.

"No, it was locked," answered Piper. "And the security alarm was on."

"No sign of forced entry," muttered the detective. He turned to Marguerite. "Was your husband expecting anyone, somebody he would have let in?"

Marguerite sniffed and shook her head. "Not that I know of," she said softly.

As Piper viewed the anguish on Marguerite's face, for some reason the memory of the men who had come into Boulangerie Bertrand her first morning in the bakery, taking measurements and pictures, flashed through her mind. Could they possibly have something to do with this?

THE UNDERSTANDING DETECTIVE AGREED THAT Marguerite and Piper could come to the police station the following day and make their formal statements.

"Is it all right if I come in around noon?" asked Marguerite. "I have a funeral to attend in the morning."

The detective looked at her skeptically.

"Bertrand and I had been planning to go to Muffuletta Mike's funeral in the morning. I know Bertrand would still want me to go and pay our respects."

"Are you sure, Marguerite?" Piper asked incredulously.

Before Marguerite could respond, they heard shouting in the corridor. One of the police officers stood at the opened door to the dumbwaiter. He yelled in fright at the sleek, coiled body and the two beady red eyes that peered out.

CHAPTER

57

THE AIR FILLED with the sound of patrons laughing and yell-ing to be heard over the jazz band's loud music. Falkner sur-veyed the Gris-Gris Bar and smiled. They all looked like they were having a good time.

With admission being charged at the door and people crowded at tables and jammed three deep at the bar, the evening was already a monetary success. Judging by the fat piles of shamrock tickets inside the individual glass bowls stationed in front of the prizes, the tricky-tray auction was also going to raise quite a bit of money for Wuzzy and his son.

It seemed as good a time as any to pick the winners. Falkner went over to the band and asked them to stop playing. He held up his arms to quiet the crowd. It didn't work.

"Hey, everyone," he called. "Is everybody having fun?"

The partygoers paid no attention, continuing to talk among themselves.

Falkner looked beseechingly at the band. "Can you do something to get their attention?" he asked.

Cecil turned to his bandmates. They'd had to do this at many parties in the Big Easy. "Let's give it to 'em, brothers," he called.

All the horn players put their instruments to their lips and blew one long, loud, screeching note. The bar patrons winced at the resulting cacophony, many putting their hands over their ears. Everyone turned to look at the band, giving Falkner the chance to make his announcement.

"We're going to call the raffle winners now. It's time to get out your tickets."

He went to the prize table and began picking shamrocks from the bowls and calling out the lucky names. Winners and their friends cheered as they won the prizes, among them a dinner for four at Bistro Sabrina, a trip to the radio station donated by Aaron Kane, a series of massages and beauty treatments at local spas and salons, a gift certificate for six psychic readings at a Royal Street fortune-teller, a tour of New Orleans donated by Falkner himself. But when he got to the brass candlesticks, Falkner slid his hand into his pocket and felt for the ticket he had taken from the top of the pile the moment Piper had walked away after depositing it in the bowl.

"Okay, folks," he called. "Next prize is these glorious candlesticks donated by Duchamps Antiques and Illuminations. Let's see who the winner is."

With Piper's ticket already clenched in his hand, Falkner stuck his fist in the bowl. He wanted Piper to have the brass candlesticks to remember him by.

He pulled the ticket from the bowl and glanced at it. Falkner opened his mouth to announce the winner just as the crowd heard the blaring sirens.

CHAPTER

58

Everyone in the bar hurried out onto Royal Street. Aaron Kane grabbed his microphone while his engineer scooped up the necessary equipment to broadcast from outside. A large crowd of St. Patrick's Day merrymakers had already gathered to gape at the activity. Police cars, emergency lights flashing, were parked in front of Boulangerie Bertrand.

Approaching people on the sidewalk and sticking his microphone in their faces, Aaron asked them what they had seen or heard.

"My friends and I were just hanging out here on the street, drinking and having a good time," said a young man wearing green Bermuda shorts and a Tulane T-shirt. "We thought the bakery was closed for the night. Then we saw a couple of women let themselves inside and turn on the lights. I didn't pay any more attention until an ambulance came hauling up the street."

Other pedestrians offered more.

"One of the paramedics came out a little while ago to get something from the back of his truck. I heard him say that they found a snake in there."

"I saw a cop shaking his head, and he told another cop he couldn't believe that the baker inside was dead. Said he'd been in the bakery buying beignets only this morning."

Aaron listened to additional accounts. He tried to keep his excitement from showing on his face. The misery inside Boulangerie Bertrand should translate to higher ratings for his radio show tonight.

When a television news van arrived, no doubt alerted by an assignment-desk police scanner, Aaron wasn't too upset. The words of the people on the street were vivid and very human— better, in Aaron's opinion, than some packaged television news report written and constructed by a reporter who was more interested in seeing himself on the air than in staying with the reactions of the average citizen. It was only when the front door of the bakery opened and a stretcher was carried out that Aaron wished he had video images to broadcast. Seeing a body bag so obviously stuffed with a corpse was a powerful and unforgettable image.

As more of the familiar yellow police tape was pulled around the crime scene, Piper and Marguerite exited the bakery. They both looked extremely pale, their appearances made more ghostly by the fact that they were covered in white powder.

Aaron pushed forward, trying to get close enough to the victim's wife and Piper to ask them some questions. But the women went straight to the black wrought-iron gate next door, quickly unlocked it, and disappeared inside.

CHAPTER

59

THE MINUTE THEY entered the apartment, Piper went to the bathroom and got two towels. She and Marguerite brushed the flour off their skin and clothes.

"Can I get you anything, Marguerite?" asked Piper. "Coffee, tea, or maybe some juice? I wish I had something stronger to offer you."

"A cup of tea would be fine," Marguerite answered in an unsteady voice. "I'll only stay for a little while, Piper, but I can't face going home yet."

Piper left Marguerite in the living area while she went to the kitchen, filled the kettle with water, and set it to boil on the stove. Then she returned to sit with Marguerite.

"Would you like to stay here with me tonight?" Piper offered.

Looking around the room, Marguerite's eyes came to rest on the French doors that led to the balcony.

"I appreciate the offer, Piper, but I think it would be even harder to stay here than it will be to stay at home. Bertrand and I were so happy when we lived in this tiny little space. We'd work hard all day downstairs, loving being together, building our dream. Then we'd come up here, relax, and enjoy each other. I can't tell you how many bottles of wine were consumed out on that balcony."

Piper smiled sadly. She didn't really know how to respond. She'd known Marguerite for only a few days, and talking on an intimate level didn't come easily. When the kettle whistled, Piper sprang from her chair, glad to have something to do.

After they finished their tea, Marguerite rose slowly to leave. "I must go home now," she said wearily. "I have to call Bertrand's family in France and let them know what's happened."

Piper nodded solemnly. "I want to help in any way I can. And I'll go with you to Muffuletta Mike's funeral tomorrow morning if you'd like."

"You don't mind?" asked Marguerite.

"Of course not," said Piper. "What time?"

"Ten o'clock at Our Lady of Guadalupe. We could meet there."

"Sure. Whatever works for you." Piper nodded, admiring Marguerite's courage and hoping that that strength would stand her in good stead in the painful days to come.

PIPER LOCKED THE DOOR BEHIND Marguerite, then immediately went to the closet, pushed back her clothes on the rack, and made sure the door to the dumbwaiter was closed tight. Though the police had called animal control to remove the snake, just the thought of the slithering reptile made Piper's skin crawl.

Next she called Jack. She was bummed when she got his voice mail. He was probably in some Manhattan bar with his FBI buddies throwing a few back for St. Paddy's Day.

She left a message.

"Jack. It's me. Just wanted to hear your voice and fill you in on the latest. Call me."

She looked at her watch. It was after eleven. Piper thought of calling her parents but decided against it. They would be beside themselves with worry if she told them what had happened. They would have to find out eventually, but what was the point of telling them now and having them spend a sleepless night? There was nothing they could do from New Jersey anyway.

Piper knew that she wasn't going to be able to fall asleep. She walked out onto the balcony and looked down. The police cars were gone, but there were still plenty of pedestrians on the street. The Gris-Gris Bar remained open.

She didn't want to be alone.

THERE WERE FEWER PEOPLE IN the bar than there had been earlier in the night. Most had gone home after the events across the street had taken much of the excitement and celebration from the evening. But when Piper entered, she was greatly relieved to be with the living, breathing human beings who remained.

Falkner was the first to notice, beckoning her to come over and join him at the bar. She gladly sat next to him. Wuzzy immediately came over and took Piper's drink order.

"I'll have a Sazerac," she said without hesitation, remembering the strength of the drink. No genteel white wine for her tonight. With a little luck, a potent cocktail would help her sleep later.

"The good news is you won those candlesticks you wanted," said Falkner.

Piper managed a weak smile.

Falkner waited until she took her first swallow of the Sazerac before beginning to ask her questions. "So? What happened over there?"

Piper shook her head and sighed. "You don't want to know. I hope I never see anything like that again."

She described going into the bakery and finding Bertrand on the floor, trying to revive him, knowing it was too late, his neck impaled by the flower nail, told them about the flour and the egg, the live snake with the beady red eyes. When Piper finished, she realized that a small audience had gathered around her, hanging on her every word.

"That's Damballah."

Piper looked up. The clarinet player was standing behind Falkner now.

"Damballah," Cecil repeated. "Those are all signs of Damballah, one of the most important of all the voodoo spirits."

Everyone turned and stared at the musician. Piper noticed that the radio-show host Aaron Kane was also in the gathering. She thought she detected a strange gleam in his eyes.

CHAPTER

60

PERFECT.

Aaron listened to the musician make the voodoo connection to Bertrand Olivier's murder and only wished his radio broadcast hadn't concluded for the night. How great it would've been to have this guy on the air, connecting the dots between the details found at the crime scene and the voodoo spirit!

Aaron knew immediately what he was going to do. He waited until Cecil drifted away from the bar and went to pack up his clarinet. Aaron followed him.

"Excuse me," he said. "I'm Aaron Kane, and I do a radio show every weeknight. I was wondering if you would be a guest on my show tomorrow evening. I think my audience would be very interested in your views."

Cecil pushed his porkpie hat farther back on his head and

studied Aaron's florid face. "I don't know," he said uncertainly.

"I think you have something very important to say," Aaron insisted. "Let's face it, voodoo and hoodoo don't get much respect. The general population has many misconceptions. You say voodoo and all they think about is sticking pins in dolls, crazy curses and spells, and people chanting, running around in circles, and whipping themselves into frenzies. You and I know there is so much more to voodoo and hoodoo than that."

Cecil listened.

"You could educate people," continued Aaron. "You'd be doing a good thing."

The uncertain expression on Cecil's face signaled he remained unconvinced.

"Listen," said Aaron. "You don't have to prepare a thing. All you have to do is show up. I'll ask you some questions, and you'll answer them any way you want. There will be some callers with questions, too, of course, but if you don't want to respond, you can just let me know and I'll carry the ball. Really. There's nothing to it. You'll be doing a public service and a service to your beliefs as well."

Aaron waited while Cecil considered his words. When the musician finally agreed, Aaron could hardly contain himself. He knew that a second murder committed by the Hoodoo Killer along with Cecil's commentary would make the ratings for tomorrow night's show spike through the roof.

Everything was playing right into his hands.

TUESDAY
MARCH 18

CHAPTER

61

IT WAS PAST MIDNIGHT.

After she had downed her second Sazerac, Piper knew she should stop. She got off the bar stool and stumbled, Falkner catching her before she fell. When he insisted on escorting her across the street back to the apartment, she accepted the offer.

She fumbled with the key, unable to slide it easily in the gate's lock. Falkner did it for her.

"Want me to come up and help you get settled?" he asked.

Piper looked at him quizzically.

"I promise, Piper. I'm a gentleman."

"Thanks," she said, "but I'll be all right."

She took the brass candlesticks he was carrying for her and climbed the stairs, getting the key into the apartment lock this time. She headed straight to the bedroom, kicking off her shoes and pulling off her jeans as she went. Collapsing onto the bed, she immediately fell asleep.

When her cell phone rang, Piper didn't hear it.

Piper was sipping a cocktail, but she couldn't taste it. Her sights were set on the tattered cloth doll. It was dancing frantically, tangled in yellow police tape. The more the doll jerked, the more snarled up it became, until, finally, the strangled doll collapsed motionless on the floor.

She watched the pool of blood seeping out slowly from beneath the doll, the wet redness growing, coloring everything in its path except for the knotted police tape. Eventually the tape began to unravel itself, and its snakelike yellow tendrils started slithering toward Piper.

She wanted to get away. Her mind willed her body to move. Nothing happened. She was paralyzed. There was no escaping.

Her fear soaring, Piper tried to call out, but no words came from her mouth. Only a desperate, whimpering sound emanated from deep inside her throat. The yellow snakes slid closer, finally merging into one that changed colors, with big red eyes springing from its head.

PIPER OPENED HER EYES. BREATHING in short, shallow gasps, she stared into the darkness and struggled to get her bearings. Slowly it came to her. She was in a bed in New Orleans. She'd been having a nightmare.

But the terrifying feeling of not being able to move was all too familiar. It was how she'd felt last month as she lay paralyzed on the hotel floor in Florida after ingesting the poisonous fish. Poison that had been purposefully fed to her. It was how she'd felt just a few days ago at the movie shoot. Though the crypt had been fake, the trapped feeling when she'd been lying enclosed inside had been all too real.

She lay there in bed now, thinking about the rest of the dream and trying to decipher its meaning. The cocktail could be the Sazeracs she'd drunk just a few hours before at the Gris-Gris Bar. The images of the yellow police tape came from both the murder scenes on Royal Street. And the red blood . . . Piper winced. She didn't even want to think about finding Bertrand that way.

But what about the cloth doll? Was her brain making the connection to words the street musician had uttered? Voodoo. Hoodoo. The only thing Piper associated with those practices were voodoo dolls, those figures that people stuck with pins when they wanted to harm someone the doll represented.

Or did the doll represent herself—tangled, terrified, and powerless as she tried to break free from a force that wanted to destroy her? Was the doll's struggle just her unconscious trying to work out the life-threatening trauma she'd endured?

She'd read somewhere that the word "nightmare" was derived from the idea of a female spirit who beset people at night while they slept. Piper also knew that spirits played a central role in voodoo and hoodoo. And, according to Cecil, the whipping that Muffuletta Mike had endured and the serpent found near Bertrand's corpse were expressions of the spirits.

As she tried to fall back asleep, Piper couldn't allow herself to think that those kinds of spirits really existed. But she did believe there was evil in the world. She had witnessed it firsthand. Evil committed by human beings. Though they might claim that spirits made them do unspeakable things, people committed the atrocities themselves.

Piper wasn't afraid of Cecil's spirits. She was terrified, though, of the person who could have perpetrated two such horrific, cold-blooded murders.

CHAPTER

62

TERRI HAD ALREADY left for work, and Vin Donovan was down in his basement man cave preparing to paint the old rocking chair. It seemed like only yesterday that he was looking down first at Robert and then at Piper as they lay in his arms while he rocked them, their little mouths moving up and down as they slept. Now he was going to be a grandfather in a few months.

He'd been surprised when Robert had told him that Zara was interested in using the rocker for their baby. Vin never figured his daughter-in-law to be the sentimental type. Everything had to be the newest and the best for Zara. In Vin's opinion she spent way too much—money the couple should be saving, especially now that they were expecting a baby. As he pried the lid off the can of white paint, Vin hoped perhaps now Zara was changing her priorities.

While he painted the rocker spindles, Vin listened to the reports coming from the small television set perched on his workbench. He looked up when the weather report came on. The map showed it would be in the high seventies in Louisiana today. Lucky Piper. Her trip to New Orleans meant that she was missing cold, dreary days up north.

Vin turned his attention back to the rocker as the newscaster began her report. Another showdown between the president and Congress, more fighting in the Middle East, Wall Street stock prices reaching an all-time high.

"Finally, in New Orleans this morning, police are investigating the murder of well-known pastry chef Bertrand Olivier."

Vin stopped painting midstroke. He rested the brush on the rim of the paint can and turned his eyes to the television again.

"Olivier, award-winning baker, cookbook author, and owner of Boulangerie Bertrand in the French Quarter, is seen in this clip from an appearance on the Food Network. His body was found on the floor of his bakery last night by his wife."

Vin's jaw dropped as he watched the video that appeared on the screen now. A vinyl body bag being wheeled out of the bakery on a stretcher. Then a woman with short dark hair was shown exiting the store. She was accompanied by a younger, taller blonde.

Piper!

Vin ran his hand through his white hair as the newscaster wrapped up.

"Details are being withheld pending investigation, but sources say police think Olivier's death may be tied to another Royal Street shopkeeper's gruesome murder last week. They are also looking at a possible voodoo connection to both crimes."

Vin snapped off the set, ran upstairs to the kitchen, and grabbed the telephone.

CHAPTER

63

PIPER WAS GROGGY with fatigue. The nightmare had left her deeply unsettled, unable to fall back into restful sleep. She'd drifted in and out all night. When she heard the muffled sound of her cell phone, at first she couldn't place it. The iPhone rang six times before she remembered she had left it in the pocket of the jeans crumpled on the floor.

The ID screen revealed that it was after nine o'clock and that the call was coming from her parents' house. It was probably her father, since her mother would be at The Icing on the Cupcake by now. For a split second, Piper considered not answering. She had to shower, dress, and meet Marguerite at the church in less than an hour. But she knew that her parents would worry if she didn't answer, especially since she hadn't spoken to them in a few days.

"Hi, Dad." Piper made an effort to sound cheerful and alert.

She could hear the urgency in her father's voice. "What's going on down there, Piper? Are you all right?"

"Yeah, I'm fine," she answered. "How are you?"

"Don't how-are-you me," Vin said sternly. "I saw you on the news this morning. What have you gotten yourself into the middle of now?"

She hadn't counted on the video taken outside the bakery last night making it to the network broadcasts.

Piper recognized the inflection in her Dad's voice. When her father was truly worried about something, his anxiety translated into harsh tones.

"I don't know, Dad. I'm not sure what I'm in the middle of, but believe me, I don't like being here."

Her voice cracked as she described what she had seen the night before. In a way it was a relief to tell her father. Even though she didn't want to worry him, she also knew he had seen a lot in his career as a New York City cop. He could take it.

"Come home, Piper," he said when she was finished.

Piper could hear Emmett, their Jack Russell terrier, yapping in the background. She'd love to be there, petting her beloved dog, secure and safe in her parents' house.

"I want to, but I can't come home, Dad, at least not for a few more days. I have to go to the police station today and give a statement, or answer questions, or whatever they want me to do. And there are two cakes to make for a couple who are getting married. With Bertrand gone, I would really be leaving them in the lurch."

Piper knew as she spoke that her father was going to understand her decision to stay in New Orleans for a while. He was all about cooperating with police investigations. He was also going to approve of his daughter's desire to honor commitments and not let down a bride and groom. But she also knew that her father was going to be plagued with worry until she was back home safe again.

She felt the same way herself.

CHAPTER

64

A TRADITIONAL CATHOLIC FUNERAL Mass for Muffuletta Mike was conducted at Our Lady of Guadalupe Church. Wearing a simple black dress and clasping her rosary beads, Ellinore listened to the familiar prayers. As always when she attended a funeral, she was reminded of Ginnie. She could still remember the ripping ache in her heart as she followed her daughter's white casket up the aisle and the years of grief that followed. Even now it hurt to think about it.

Ellinore doubted she would have been able to survive her daughter's death without Nettie. Her steady, loving presence in the house had provided Ellinore with comfort. When Ellinore lay unable to move in her bed, Nettie quietly came in and covered her. When Ellinore could barely eat, Nettie made soothing broths and soups, sometimes sitting on the edge of Ellinore's bed and spooning the nourishment into her mouth. When Ellinore wept, Nettie held her.

It was unbelievable to think that Nettie wasn't going to be with her anymore. But it was another heartache that must be borne. The idea that voodoo had been practiced in her house absolutely repulsed Ellinore. Nettie had defiled her home and destroyed the trust Ellinore had in her.

As Muffuletta Mike's casket was carried out, Ellinore stood with a heavy heart and watched his wife and son walking behind it. The son supported his mother, faces etched with grief. Once they passed, other mourners started streaming from the pews behind them.

Ellinore was touched to see that so many of the Royal Street family had shown up. The haberdasher, the jeweler, the candy-store owner, even the fortune-teller—all of them were there. Ellinore was impressed as she observed Marguerite Olivier, only the day after her own husband was killed. She was accompanied by a tall, pretty blonde whom Ellinore didn't know.

Her nephew, Falkner, barely nodded to her as he passed. So did the owner of the bar next to her shop. Ellinore suspected that both men might be wishing they were attending *her* funeral today. Having her out of the picture would leave her antique shop wide open for Wuzzy Queen's bar expansion. And Falkner had been livid when she told him he wasn't going to inherit her estate. He demanded to know who was, but Ellinore hadn't told him. There would be time enough for Falkner to resent Sabrina after Ellinore was gone.

Sabrina and Leo stopped when they saw Ellinore and escorted her out of the church. The music from the pipe organ inside was replaced by the slow, somber strains of "The Old Rugged Cross" played by the jazz musicians gathered on the sidewalk. Ellinore watched as pallbearers slid the casket into the back of the black hearse that would carry the body the short distance around the block to the cemetery. Mourners gathered behind the hearse to follow on foot, escorting Muffuletta Mike to his final resting place.

The sound of banjos, horns, and drums filled the air. Ellinore went by the jazz musicians on her way to join the other walkers. As she passed the clarinetist in the porkpie hat, she thought that he looked familiar.

She shivered when she realized who he was. Nettie's brother Cecil was glaring at her over his clarinet.

CHAPTER

65

*The sign beside the front door of the church proclaimed that con-
fessions were offered a half hour before every Mass. How welcome it would be to lay down this awful burden in the confessional,
do penance, and be forgiven. If only it were that simple.*

*As if telling a priest could actually cleanse the soul and make
things right again. Nice in theory for the sinner. Not so comforting for
the person sinned against. Shouldn't the victim of the sin have some say
about whether the sinner was forgiven?*

*And wasn't one of the tenets of the sacrament to "go and sin no
more"? If the sinner went into the confessional knowing full well that
there was another deadly sin planned for the immediate future, God
would be aware of that, too. He'd know that the sinner wasn't acting
in good faith.*

Maybe after the last murder was finished, maybe then it would be worth it to cover all bets and go to confession. But no matter what penance was assigned, it was hard to actually believe that God would ever forgive the bloody atrocities committed in the name of voodoo.

CHAPTER

66

THE JAZZ MUSICIANS finished playing "The Old Rugged Cross" and began "Just a Closer Walk with Thee" as the mourners marched closer to the cemetery. Piper was amazed at the procession. While she was solemn and worried about the terrible events of the last week, she was also aware that she was witnessing something that few people other than New Orleans residents ever experienced.

"These songs are so moving," Piper said into Marguerite's ear as they followed the band.

"The funeral dirges help remind us of the ups and downs of life," said Marguerite, holding a tissue to the corner of her eye. "But wait till later. They'll be playing 'When the Saints Go Marching In' or 'Li'l Liza Jane,' and people will be dancing under decorated umbrellas and waving white handkerchiefs with the idea that life isn't over at death. The jazz funeral celebrates the fact that the person who died is free now to dance on the other side. I'm trying to remember that."

Piper reached over and patted the woman's shoulder. "I really admire how you're handling this, Marguerite. You're incredibly brave."

"Not really," said Marguerite. "I'm just trying to do the best I can. I'm determined to carry on, Piper."

Reaching the cemetery entrance, the pallbearers pulled the casket from the back of the hearse and rocked the coffin to the beat of the music.

"What are they doing?" asked Piper, incredulous.

"They are making sure Muffuletta Mike has one last dance," answered Marguerite.

Hoisting the coffin up on their shoulders, the pallbearers passed under the tall iron cross that topped the gate. Piper and Marguerite followed with the rest of the mourners.

As she walked along the path made of sand, gravel, and crushed shells, Piper could see why New Orleans cemeteries were called "Cities of the Dead." The aboveground monuments and crypts looked like buildings and houses lined up along narrow streets. The taller wall vaults, housing dozens of tombs, were the city's skyscrapers. Walking deeper into the maze of the crammed cemetery, Piper began to feel squeamish and claustrophobic.

Piper stopped. "Marguerite?" she asked. "Would you mind going on without me? I'm going to wait for a bit."

Marguerite searched Piper's face. "Are you all right, Piper? You're flushed."

"I'll be fine, really. I just need to take a break. Go ahead. I'll catch up with you."

"All right. But if you don't show up in a few minutes, I'm coming back to get you."

The morning sun had risen in the sky and was shining down strongly, attracted by the whiteness of the tombs. Piper cursed herself for failing to wear her wide-brimmed straw hat. She separated herself from the other mourners and looked for a shady place, finding an area where a tall wall vault blocked the burning rays. She welcomed the noticeably cooler air there.

From her sheltered spot, she could still see the people filing along the path on their way to watch Muffuletta Mike's interment. She noticed Aaron Kane at the same time he turned his head and noticed her. Piper groaned inwardly as she saw him break from the group and walk over. The last thing she needed right now was the sloppy smoocher from the St. Patrick's Day parade.

"Don't worry. I have no intention of kissing you," he said, as if reading her mind.

"That's a relief," said Piper.

"What's the matter? Aren't you feeling well?" Aaron asked with concern in his voice as he mopped his own brow. "I have a bottle of water with me, if you'd like it. I've been to some funerals here before, and these cemeteries can feel like rotisseries."

Piper hesitated, not wanting to take anything from the man, but she decided to accept the water. She was overheated and feeling weak. It would be stupid not to take the unopened bottle just because she had an uneasy feeling about the man offering it.

"I fear we got off to a bad start, Piper," said Aaron as he

watched her drink. "I hope I didn't offend you. The kissing cane is one of our St. Patrick's Day traditions."

Piper took the bottle from her mouth and nodded, softening a little. "No harm done," she said. She pointed deeper into the cemetery. "How long do you think this will take?"

"Not too long," said Aaron. "They'll say some prayers and file by the tomb, and that will be it."

Piper took another swallow and looked around at the nearby vaults. "Each one is marked with one family's name, but they don't look large enough to hold entire families."

"Ah, that's the ingenious part. One body at a time is deposited in the vault. Then the sun does the rest, beating down on what is essentially a brick-and-concrete oven. Over a year's time, the remains disintegrate to almost nothing."

"Like cremation," said Piper.

"Pretty much, except there are no flames and it takes longer. But it's a very efficient system. Before we got here today, the closure tablet was removed from the front of Mike's tomb and the vault inside was cleaned out of what might be left of past coffins. Any human remains in there were bagged, tagged, and put in the lower section of the vault to make room for Mike."

Piper's imagination wandered, from Muffuletta Mike's body going into a small, dark, hot place to memories of her panicked experience inside the tomb on the movie set to her terrifying paralysis after being poisoned. Suddenly she couldn't catch her breath, everything started to swim around her, and she sank to the ground.

SOMEONE WAS SHAKING HER. SHE heard her name.

"Piper. Piper!"

Slowly, so slowly, she opened her eyes. The light hurt, and she closed them again. Her hand was being rubbed, and something wet and cool was on her forehead. The voice was gentler this time.

"Piper, *please,* wake up."

She raised her eyelids and tried to focus. There were dark figures looming over her. The first one she recognized was Falkner. He stood above her—protectively, she felt.

"There you go," he said. "You're going to be all right."

Piper turned her head and saw Marguerite kneeling beside her. She was the one stroking her hand. Piper tried to smile at her, but she couldn't.

"I'm all right," she whispered. "I don't know what happened."

"You fainted and were out for a bit," Marguerite said. "What matters is that you're okay."

"You shouldn't be worrying about me," said Piper, her voice growing stronger. "You have enough to worry about already."

"Never mind that," said Marguerite. "We're going to get you to a doctor. Do you think you can get up?"

"I think I can," said Piper. "And really, I don't need a doctor."

Falkner and Wuzzy helped lift her. She wobbled at first, but after taking a few steps she began to feel steadier on her feet. She noticed Aaron Kane smiling at her encouragingly.

As they got closer to the cemetery gates, the jazz music grew louder.

"When the Saints Go Marching In."

The former mourners were now dancers, twisting and

twirling in the bright sunshine, the living celebrating the eternal life of Muffuletta Mike.

Marguerite and the others stood with her as Falkner tried to hail a cab. Piper noticed that Sabrina and Leo were nearby, talking to an older woman Piper didn't recognize. But she heard the woman speaking loudly over the music.

"All right, come in today, but I won't have you coming in the rest of the week, Sabrina. A bride has too much to do. I'm only going to be open from noon till five this week anyway."

CHAPTER

67

AFTER THE FUNERAL Cecil went straight to his place. He put his clarinet case down on the floor, peeled off his sweat-drenched shirt, and went to the kitchen and took a cold Fanta from the refrigerator. Hot and tired, he quickly gulped down the orange soda and then angrily crushed the can.

When he saw Ellinore Duchamps in front of the church, it was all he could do to keep himself from putting down his clarinet and spitting in her face. The way she had treated Nettie, after all those years of loyal service, was just not right! As Cecil thought about his sister's tearful account of Ellinore's callous dismissal, the resentment rose in his chest.

What had Nettie really done wrong? She hadn't hurt anyone or stolen anything. She had merely practiced her religion, just as

Ellinore practiced hers. Even if Ellinore didn't believe in voodoo, she should have respected Nettie's right to her own beliefs.

Ellinore was wicked. But Cecil's experience told him that eventually people paid for their sins. He had to believe that. Otherwise he would drive himself crazy with thoughts about the unfairness and inequities in life.

He lay down on the old couch and closed his eyes. Cecil thought more about the funeral. He wondered if Muffuletta Mike was pleased, wherever he was. He could be in a heavenlike place or he could be doomed to live on earth as a bodiless spirit. To Cecil it wasn't clear what fate awaited Mike.

In his mind Cecil went over the experiences he'd had with Mike. Mike had made sandwiches for Cecil, but he made them grudgingly. Cecil knew that Mike couldn't wait to get him out of the shop whenever he came in.

Cecil didn't like the way Mike treated his son either. Many times Cecil had heard Mike berating Tommy, who clearly hated working in the shop and, according to his father, had no real aptitude for it. Cecil felt sorry for the kid. When Tommy had asked Cecil to put together the jazz funeral, Cecil had done it for the boy, not for his father.

But when word got to Cecil that Mike had complained to the cops about him, wanting him to move and play somewhere else, Cecil's opinion about Mike was sealed. How Mike wanted to act in his own place was one thing. Trying to restrain Cecil from playing on the corner across the street from the sandwich shop was quite another. Cecil had owned that spot for years. It belonged to him, tied not with a formal lease but with tradition. His father had staked out that corner. Cecil could still feel his father's spirit there. Cecil knew it was where he belonged.

Muffuletta Mike didn't think so.

In the end, Cecil knew, people got what they deserved.

And now Bertrand Olivier was dead, too.

Cecil got up from the couch. He wished he had never agreed to go on Aaron Kane's radio show tonight. He wasn't only concerned about what he was going to say and if he'd be able to do his religion justice with his words. He was also worried that now, with two murders on Royal Street, his talking about voodoo could implicate him with the police. They were surely looking for someone to pin the bloody crimes on, and he might seem like a good candidate.

CHAPTER

68

MARGUERITE INSISTED ON accompanying Piper upstairs.

"Are you sure you won't see a doctor, Piper?" she asked as they entered the apartment.

Piper shook her head. "No, really, I'm fine. I just want to lie down for a little while."

Marguerite looked skeptical, but she acquiesced. "All right, but there's no way you're coming with me to talk to the police," she declared. "I'll tell them what happened at the cemetery. They can interview you another time."

Piper didn't protest. She felt washed out, and her eyes burned. Marguerite and she both had seen the same horrible things last night. She doubted she'd have anything to add to what Marguerite would describe. Though Piper was more than willing to talk to the police, it didn't have to be right now. Better later, when she was feeling stronger and more alert.

But she did want to talk to Marguerite about something else. Sabrina and Leo's wedding celebration on the *Natchez* was only two days away, with the reception at the restaurant on the following day. If Piper was to make the cakes, she had to be able to use the kitchen and ovens downstairs in the bakery. Would the police still have the area closed off as a crime scene?

"You know, you're right," said Marguerite. "I hadn't even thought about the wedding. I'm determined that the business Bertrand and I built will go on, but I just assumed the bakery would be closed until after his funeral. . . ." Her voice trailed off, and her eyes filled with tears.

"Oh, Marguerite," said Piper, distressed. "I'm so sorry. Really I am. I hate bringing up such a trivial matter at a time like this."

"I know you're sorry, Piper." Marguerite straightened her posture and wiped away the dampness at her eyes. "But of course. Bertrand would want us to fulfill his commitment to Sabrina and Leo. I'll talk to the police about it. I don't see why they can't make sure to go through at least the kitchen today for any evidence. They'd probably want to do that as soon as possible anyway. If they want us to keep the rest of the place closed for a while, I couldn't care less."

WHEN MARGUERITE LEFT FOR THE police station, Piper went to the bedroom and lay down. She breathed deeply, in and out, trying to soothe herself, attempting to practice the meditation techniques she'd learned in her yoga classes. Breathe in through the nose. Exhale long and deeply through the mouth, releasing toxicity and tension. She imagined herself looking out at the calm, clear waters of the Gulf of Mexico, feeling a cool breeze blowing soothingly. Piper started to drift off to sleep.

Her nap was interrupted by her ringing cell phone. She answered immediately when she saw the name on the screen.

"Oh, Jack. I've been wanting to talk to you," she said with relief. "I tried you last night. Where were you?"

"Out with some of the guys," he said. "The bar was noisy, and I didn't hear my phone. I called you back on my way home in the cab, but you didn't answer. I had to testify in court this morning about one of my cases. This is the first minute I've had to call you again."

She pictured him getting up early, showering, shaving, and dressing, all the while going over his testimony in his mind. He probably didn't have the television on. He wouldn't have heard the news.

"It doesn't matter," answered Piper. "I'm just so glad to hear your voice."

"What's wrong, Pipe?"

"Why do you always assume something is wrong?"

"Don't answer my question with another question, okay? Something's wrong, Pipe. What is it?"

She told him. About finding Bertrand murdered, about the flour and the snake in the dumbwaiter, the flower nail and the CPR, about the jazz funeral and the fainting episode in the cemetery.

"I'm hanging up now and making you a plane reservation to come home on the next available flight," Jack said when she was finished. "I'll call you right back."

"No, Jack. I can't come home yet. I can't abandon Marguerite or leave the couple getting married in the lurch. It's Tuesday. I'll come home Friday night as soon as I finish the cake for their wedding reception. I promise."

"I don't think you get it, Piper. That first murder was committed down the street. The victim was somebody you didn't know. Voodoo, hoodoo, whatever is going on down there, Bertrand's murder puts you right in the middle of it now. That's a good enough reason to get yourself out of there and fast. And while we're at it, have you ever fainted before in your entire life?"

"No," Piper said softly. "But even my father understands why I can't come home yet. Why can't you?"

"I get why you think you should stay, Piper, but I think you should see a doctor, a shrink or something. You've been through a lot—that nightmare last month in Florida—it's taking its toll, physically and mentally. The world will go on if you don't make a wedding cake. I'd come down there right now and bring you back myself if I didn't have to be in court to testify again this afternoon."

"Don't talk to me like I'm a child, Jack."

"Well, then don't act like one, Piper. I just don't think you understand how serious this is."

CHAPTER

69

THE GRIS-GRIS BAR was nearly empty. For once Wuzzy was glad that business was slow. Between Bertrand's murder the night before and Muffuletta Mike's funeral that morning, he wished he could have taken the rest of the day off to spend with Connor. All that death had left him drained and reminded him of how short life could be. But somebody had to tend bar for the rest of the afternoon. Plus, the place was trashed from the fund-raiser.

As he swept the scuffed wooden floor, Wuzzy glanced up at the ceiling and the old leather pouches that hung from it. When he'd bought the place, the last owner had explained that the gris-gris bags were recipes for magic, good and bad. For white magic the gris-gris bags and their ingredients should be hung above a door or on a wall or from a ceiling. For black magic the bags could be left on a doorstep as a warning.

Wuzzy had stopped himself from rolling his eyes at the time. He wanted the sale to go through and didn't want to offend the owner, who clearly thought there was something to the gris-gris idea. Wuzzy wondered if the poor guy should have taken some of his gris-gris bags with him when he left and hung them in his own house. The former bar owner had died in a car accident shortly after Wuzzy took possession of the bar.

With the floor clear, Wuzzy went back behind the counter to take stock of the liquor bottles that were near empty. As he entered into his computer a list of the brands he needed to replace, Falkner came sauntering in. He was smiling broadly.

"I counted it all up, Wuz," he said excitedly as he took a seat on a high stool. "We raised enough to buy that electric wheelchair. Between the booze and that raffle, we really cleaned up, man."

"That's great, Falkner. Just great." Wuzzy shook his head in wonder. "I can't tell you how much I appreciate all you did, what everybody did, for Connor and for me."

Wuzzy's words were sincere. He was truly grateful. Having the payment for Connor's motorized chair was a big relief and a great gift. But at the same time, Wuzzy was already worried about where the money was going to come from for all the future expenses that would inevitably mount over the lifetime of his handicapped child.

If only he could expand the bar.

CHAPTER

70

PIPER HATED THAT her conversation with Jack had ended so poorly. She knew in her heart that he reacted so strongly just because he cared about her and was concerned about her safety. She wished she hadn't gotten angry with him.

But it bothered her that Jack didn't trust her to be able to handle the situation she was in. She was a grown woman and could take care of herself. While she appreciated Jack's concern, he had to respect that she was going to do what she thought was right.

He had made one salient point, though. She was definitely going to make a doctor's appointment when she got home. Deep down Piper knew that she probably hadn't fainted from the heat in the cemetery. It had been warm there, and the sun had been beating down strongly, but she'd been in much hotter weather than that many times before. Rather it had been thinking about Muffuletta Mike being shoved into the darkness of his crypt and then remembering the panicked, claustrophobic feeling in the fake tomb for the movie, which harked back to the paralysis in the hotel room in Florida, that had sent her mind reeling. It was as though her system couldn't take the overload of fear that coursed through it at the memories.

She still recollected it so clearly. The day for her cousin's wedding had been glorious. Piper had been so happy. At least her cousin's wedding day was perfect. The days leading up to it had been marred by tragedy—and the murder of a bridesmaid.

The bride and groom had spoken their vows beneath the shining sun on a soft white beach. The ceremony was followed by a wedding brunch.

Piper had been famished and quickly ate the bowl of gazpacho that had been set out as a first course. She'd thought the cold soup tasted odd. She'd never had gazpacho with fish in it before.

Soon after, her head started to ache, but she thought the sun's blinding glare was to blame. When she went to her hotel room to get sunglasses, she'd lain down to rest. She'd used the time to post a picture of the newlyweds on Facebook and then scrolled through her page. A response to a picture she'd posted a few days earlier had helped her put the pieces together. She knew who the killer was.

But as she'd tried to rise from the bed and go for help, Piper felt the room spin around her and she crumpled to the floor. Her body was paralyzed!

Even more terrifying, she couldn't catch her breath. She managed only short, shallow gulps, never feeling that the oxygen was actually getting to her lungs. She was suffocating! Piper had been sure she was going to die.

She hadn't died, though. Jack had saved her, giving her mouth-to-mouth and confirming for doctors that she'd remarked that the gazpacho had tasted fishy. It turned out that the killer had laced her soup with toxic puffer fish.

The life-support measures that kept her alive in the hospital had been followed by days of recuperation. She still wasn't quite a hundred percent physically.

But her body wasn't the problem now. Piper realized that her mental and emotional well-being was far more battered.

When she returned north, she would find someone to talk to about all of it. But first she had to get through the next few days. Tomorrow she had to bake the layers for the wedding cake for Sabrina and Leo's *Natchez* wedding cruise. Thursday she would decorate it and make the smaller cake for Friday's nuptial dinner. Friday morning she would decorate that smaller cake, and then she could fly home.

It was important that she rest and get a good night's sleep so she could hit the ground running in the morning. Piper decided to order in some dinner, watch television, and then turn in.

CHAPTER

71

JACK FINISHED HIS testimony in federal court, relieved to be through for the day. The defense attorney had hammered him, determined to find holes in Jack's account of the defendant's alleged criminal actions. Jack was glad he'd stayed cool on the stand. It hadn't been easy.

The facts were straightforward as far as Jack was concerned. Agents of the FBI's Joint Terrorism Task Force had conducted their investigation over months and months, trailing a foreign national with connections to al-Qaeda who had come to the United States for the purpose of conducting a terrorist attack on U.S. soil. Seeking out al-Qaeda contacts in the United States and attempting to recruit other individuals to form a terrorist cell, he screwed himself when one of his recruits turned out to be an FBI source.

Long story short: An FBI undercover agent supplied the terrorist with a thousand pounds of purported explosives. Agents kept him under surveillance as he stored the material, purchased components for the bomb's detonators, and assembled what he believed to be a massively destructive explosive device. The Federal Bureau of Investigation was ready and waiting when the guy tried to detonate his useless bomb in Rockefeller Center. The terrorist now faced charges of attempting to use a weapon of mass destruction and attempting to provide material support to al-Qaeda.

Slam dunk.

Or it should be.

Jack believed that everyone should get a fair trial and was innocent until proven guilty. That was the American way. But thousands and thousands of dollars and man-hours were being spent. The bill to the taxpayers was mounting. As far as Jack was concerned, the terrorist was getting far better treatment than he deserved from the country he had committed himself to destroying.

Loosening his tie the minute he exited the courtroom, Jack wished he could go straight to his apartment, kick off his shoes, and pour himself a beer. But he had to go back to the office. His colleagues would want an update.

As he walked through Cadman Plaza on his way to the subway that would take him from Brooklyn back to Manhattan, Jack had another task he wanted to accomplish. He was going to call the Bureau's field office in New Orleans. He needed to find out what was really going on down there.

The top investigative priority of the FBI was protecting the nation from terrorist attack. Jack was determined to play his part in keeping America safe. That was how he chose to spend his professional life. But his heart was in New Orleans right now.

He regretted that he had come down so hard on Piper during their phone conversation, but he wasn't about to apologize for his plea to her. He loved Piper, and he wanted her to be safe. Making a couple of wedding cakes wasn't worth risking her life.

Why couldn't she see that?

CHAPTER

72

Aaron adjusted his headphones and pulled the microphone on his desk a little closer as he waited for the signal from the engineer to begin speaking.

"Good evening. I'm Aaron Kane, and tonight we have Cecil Gregson with us. Cecil is a jazz musician and a voodoo practitioner, and he has agreed to answer your questions about voodoo and the hoodoo murderer loose on Royal Street."

"I've never fully understood what voodoo is, Cecil," said Aaron. "What is it that you actually believe?"

Aaron looked at Cecil encouragingly and nodded to him.

Cecil cleared his throat. "Sure, I'll take a shot at explaining it to you," he said in a soft, smooth voice. "Our beliefs are the same as the Ten Commandments. In the voodoo religion, there is only one God. We believe in Christ and the many loa who are also the descendants of the one God and can carry prayers to him. Each loa has its own work that it does for the people. The answer to every problem that exists is with the loa under God."

"Thank you, Cecil," said Aaron, smiling at him. "I understand that the loa are equated with Catholic saints. Is that right?"

"Yes, sir. Voodoo is rooted in Africa, and it was brought to the New World by African men and women who were enslaved. The Catholic saints are used to represent the loa because slave masters forbade their slaves from pursuing voodoo as a religion. Any slave caught practicing any religion other than Catholicism was punished, big time. So the slaves would pretend to pray to the images of Catholic saints while in their hearts they were praying to their African spirits. We still do that today."

"So yesterday was St. Patrick's Day. Is St. Patrick associated with a loa?" asked Aaron, knowing exactly where he wanted his question to lead.

"Yes, sir. Damballah, the sky spirit, is associated with St. Patrick, who drove the snakes out of Ireland. Damballah's symbol is the serpent."

"I see," said Aaron. "Cecil, you were with me at the Gris-Gris Bar on Royal Street last night when we heard the news of Bertrand Olivier's murder across the street, weren't you?"

"Yes, sir. I was."

"And we heard an eyewitness to the crime scene describe what she had seen, didn't we?"

"Yes, sir. We did."

"Why don't you tell us what she said, Cecil, and what you thought when you heard it? Will you?"

Cecil looked at the radio host uncertainly. "I'm not sure about that, Mr. Kane," he said.

"She described that a mound of white flour with an egg on top was found by the body, along with a snake. Isn't that right?"

"I guess so, yeah," said Cecil, twisting his hands in front of him on the desk.

"That's right, Cecil," said Aaron. "Tell us what went through your mind when she mentioned those details."

Cecil stayed quiet.

"It's all right, Cecil," Aaron said reassuringly. "It's a free country. You can think and say whatever you want, can't you?"

Taking a deep breath, Cecil answered, "I thought of Damballah. White is his color, flour and an egg are his offerings, and his symbol is the snake."

The lights started popping on the telephone lines in the radio studio, full of callers who wanted to chime in on the topic of the Royal Street murders. Aaron's producer screened each one before putting the caller on the air. While Cecil answered their questions as best he could, Aaron sat back for a while and reveled in the success of his plan. The Hoodoo Killer was saving his professional life.

As they neared the end of the show, Aaron took over again. "I want to thank Cecil Gregson for being with us tonight and enlightening us on such a fascinating yet disturbing subject. One last thing before we go, Cecil. Tomorrow is St. Joseph's Day. Can you tell us if there is a voodoo loa associated with St. Joseph?"

Cecil shifted uncomfortably in his chair. "Yes, sir," he said. "Loko, the guardian of the deepest secret, the secret of initiation. No secret is unknown to Loko."

"And what is Loko's symbol?" asked Aaron.

Looking as if he couldn't wait to escape, Cecil answered, "Loko shows himself as the butterfly."

CHAPTER

73

PIPER WAS STRETCHED out watching television when the phone rang. Her parents were calling. She braced herself for a lecture.

"Piper? It's Mom. Guess what Daddy and I just saw? Your dog-food commercial!"

Piper sat up. It had been two months since she shot the commercial in Los Angeles. Finally it was airing.

"Really?" she asked.

"Yes. We were watching *Law & Order,* and up you came."

Piper thought quickly. *Law & Order* wasn't on NBC Tuesday night.

"What channel did you see it on?" she asked.

She heard her mother calling to her father. "What channel is this, Vin?"

Piper could hear him answer back. "Thirty-eight."

That meant it was a rerun on cable, not network prime time, Piper thought with disappointment. Network prime time meant heftier residual checks. Oh, well, it could air again and again, hopefully on the traditional networks, too. The more the better. Her checking account was desperately in need of an infusion.

"Great, Mom. I'm glad you guys saw it," said Piper. "But why are you up? You're usually in bed by nine."

"Daddy told me about what happened to you down there, and I couldn't fall asleep. It's so terrifying. But I didn't call you before because I didn't want to add to the fear. That wouldn't help anybody. Daddy told me why you think you have to stay."

Piper could picture it. Her mother lying in bed, eyes opened, worrying about her daughter. She'd gotten up and gone downstairs for reassurance and comfort, joining her night-owl husband, who was watching his favorite show. As a former cop, he loved to watch *Law & Order,* reruns or not, and point out any inaccuracies he found.

"I *do* have to stay, Mom," said Piper. "But I've already booked a flight to come home Friday night. Don't worry about me, *please.*"

THE LOCAL NEWS CAME ON at ten. The top story was about the murders on Royal Street. It recapped Muffuletta Mike's and Bertrand's murders and featured an interview with the New Orleans mayor.

"Our police department is using all its considerable resources to investigate. The French Quarter is a treasured part of our city, for our residents and for the millions of visitors who come here each year. Tourism pumps billions of dollars into our economy. We can't afford to have people being afraid to walk the streets of the Big Easy."

Turning off the television, Piper went into the bathroom to brush her teeth. As she looked at herself in the mirror, she thought about her parents and how lucky she was to have them. They drove her crazy sometimes, but she never doubted for a minute that they had anything but her best interests at heart.

She looked forward to getting back to New Jersey, to them . . . and to Jack. He hadn't called since their tiff on the phone, but she hadn't called him either. They were just going to have to agree to disagree.

Taking two Tylenol PM tablets, Piper turned off the light. Sleep did not come quickly. She tossed and turned, growing increasingly frustrated. She *had* to get a good night's rest. She had lots to do downstairs in the bakery in the morning. Marguerite had called to say that the police had cleared the kitchen for her use.

Thinking that some music might help her drift off, Piper turned on the radio that sat on the bedside table. She twisted the dial, trying to find a station to her liking. When she heard the words "hoodoo murderer on Royal Street," she stopped.

At first she found the discussion on Aaron Kane's show interesting, learning things she didn't know about voodoo, its history and belief system. But when Aaron began describing the eyewitness at the Gris-Gris Bar who had been at the murder scene, Piper felt her face grow hot.

He was talking about *her*!

How stupid she'd been! What could she have been thinking? Maybe the details she had blabbed for anyone standing around the bar to hear were bits of information the cops didn't want the public to know. She knew that the police often withheld the details of a case.

The last thing she wanted was to do damage to the police investigation!

CHAPTER

74

The butterflies arrived today, just as the company had promised they would. Five dozen painted ladies, a bit smaller than the monarchs but less expensive and just as showy. According to the company Web site, painted ladies would linger around the release area for hours.

Not that they were going to be released outside. All the lights would have to be turned on in the shop. The fluttering creatures didn't fly in the dark.

The directions were easy to follow. Cut open the cardboard delivery box and remove the Styrofoam lid. Take out the ice pack in the shipping container and replace it with a Ziploc bag full of ice cubes. Then put the Styrofoam lid back on the cooler, leaving a small ventilation gap to provide the butterflies with fresh air until the time of release. Keeping them cool would ensure that they slept.

Who knew butterflies were cold-blooded insects and at cool temperatures entered a natural state of hibernation?

That was all there was to it. Until tomorrow.

WEDNESDAY
MARCH 19
ST. JOSEPH'S DAY

CHAPTER

75

PIPER WALKED AROUND the corner to the alley behind Boulangerie Bertrand. She entered through the rear door, unsure if the police had finished their search for clues in the rest of the bakery.

At first she was puzzled by the dark smudges all over the bakery kitchen. On the white walls, on the gleaming stainless-steel ovens, on the light wood of the worktable. Then she realized what they were. The patches of fine, black powder were the residue left by the police when they dusted for fingerprints.

She wondered what they had found. Surely the place was covered with Bertrand's and Marguerite's prints. She hoped the investigators would find others. Then it occurred to Piper that her own fingerprints must be all over the place, too.

They couldn't possibly look at her as a suspect, could they?

Between that thought and the knowledge that she had indiscreetly chatted about aspects of the case that had now been broadcast on the radio all over New Orleans, Piper's heart raced. Of course she was going to be a person of interest to the police. Once they went to Aaron and questioned him about the woman he'd described on his show as revealing details of the crime scene, he was sure to identify her.

Piper tried to stay focused on the task at hand. She turned her attention to scrubbing the worktable clean.

After turning on the oven and setting it at 350 degrees, Piper assembled the ingredients for the red velvet cake. Cocoa powder, cake flour, sugar, salt, canola oil, eggs, red gel-paste food coloring, vanilla extract, buttermilk, baking soda, and white vinegar.

As she whisked together the flour, salt, and cocoa powder, Piper was amazed that she was actually making a cake as if nothing had happened, when less than forty-eight hours ago a human being had been killed here. It was frightening and eerie. She tried to keep her mind on the task before her.

In a larger bowl, she mixed the sugar and oil on medium speed with the industrial-size electric mixer. She added eggs, one at a time, mixing well after each addition. Food coloring and vanilla followed.

She measured out the flour and poured it into the bowl in three batches, alternating with buttermilk. The last step was combining the baking soda and vinegar and adding it to the batter.

By the time she was finished, Piper had decided. She was going to the police before they came to her.

CHAPTER

76

FALKNER HAD BEEN barely able to look at his aunt at the funeral. Since she'd informed him about her plans at dinner Sunday night, he'd been sick. He'd gone through the motions of doing what he needed to do for the successful fund-raiser at the Gris-Gris Bar, and he paid his respects to Muffuletta Mike, all the while trying to wrap his mind around the implications.

He wouldn't inherit the grand mansion in the Garden District. Though he had never pictured himself living in the old mausoleum, he knew what the place should bring on the open market. With some good investment advice and a little luck, the proceeds would ensure that he could live comfortably for the rest of his life.

Falkner sat at his desk, trying to work on his dissertation. Today he was tackling "Mary, Mary Quite Contrary."

Mary, Mary, quite contrary
How does your garden grow?
With silver bells and cockleshells
And pretty maids all in a row.

It turns out the sweet little rhyme may actually have been written about mass executions. The Mary was believed to refer to "Bloody Mary," the Catholic queen who did a masterful job of filling graveyards with Protestants. The "garden" in the rhyme referred either to a cemetery or to the fact that Mary had failed to produce an heir: Her garden was bare.

There was more. The "silver bells and cockleshells" were instruments of torture! "Silver bell" was the nickname for a thumbscrew, and cockleshells were believed to be torture devices attached to the genitals. "Pretty maids all in a row" could refer to either stillborn children or a contraption called a maiden, used to behead people.

Nice.

Falkner reminded himself to tell Wuzzy not to read the rhyme to Connor.

Exhaling with disgust, he closed his laptop. He felt doomed. The academic life was the one he had chosen, though he had discovered he wasn't all that well suited for it. He wasn't enjoying the research and found the writing sheer agony. If and when he became a professor, he'd be expected to publish scholarly articles, meaning he'd be in for more of the same.

His plan had been to have a teaching job at one of the city's colleges, not getting paid on a grand scale but having freedom and time off to pursue his other interests, in whatever fashion he desired. The money from Ellinore's estate would have allowed him to do that. But that plan was crumbling now.

He supposed he wasn't too old to change career paths. People far more advanced in years did it all the time. But Falkner didn't want to work that hard.

Lighting a cigarette, he squinted as he blew out the first puff of smoke. The nicotine made his brain work faster, better. He was sure of it, especially as the new thought occurred to him.

Ellinore had said she *was* changing her will, not that she *had* actually changed it. Nothing was final yet. There was still time to get her to reconsider.

77

PIPER INSERTED A cake tester into the middle of each layer. When it came out clean, she took the pans from the oven and put them on wire racks to cool. Then she grabbed her cell phone and called Marguerite.

"I don't want to bother you," said Piper. "But I just wanted to see how you're doing and if there's anything I can help you with."

"I'm all right, I guess," Marguerite answered. "I just got off the phone with the undertaker."

"Oh. Did you decide when the funeral will be?"

"Bertrand's body will be cremated," Marguerite said. "His ashes will be sent back to France, where he was born. That's what Bertrand would want. We'll have some sort of memorial service for him here at a later date."

Piper couldn't help but be a bit relieved. She didn't relish the thought of going to another cemetery anytime soon.

"I just took the red velvet cakes out of the oven for the *Natchez* wedding celebration tomorrow night," she said, wanting to offer something positive.

"Oh, that's good, Piper. I really appreciate that you did that," said Marguerite. "I wouldn't want Sabrina and Leo disappointed at what should be such a happy time for them. Life has to go on, doesn't it?" Before Piper could answer, Marguerite went on to ask another question. "How did the place look when you got there?"

"I came in through the back and haven't gone out to the hallway or the selling area," Piper explained. "I didn't want to."

"I can certainly understand that," Marguerite said. "I'm dreading doing that myself. But you can if you want. The police are finished in there, too."

"Well, I can see they've done a pretty thorough job in the kitchen. There was black powder all over the place where they dusted for fingerprints. I've cleaned up some of it and will get to the rest later when I get back. I'm going over to the police station now and see if they will take my statement. Can you tell me where to go?"

"It's just up the block," said Marguerite. "It's at 334 Royal Street."

THE DETECTIVE WHO LISTENED TO Piper gave no indication of what he thought. His face remained expressionless as he took notes while she described what she had seen in the bakery hallway.

Her parents had instilled in her the belief that it was always better to tell the truth, no matter how uncomfortable it might be. Piper bit her lower lip as she summoned up the courage to tell the detective about the radio show.

"I'm afraid I've made a big mistake," she said.

The detective looked directly into her eyes. "Really? How so?"

"That night I went to bed and tried to fall sleep, but I couldn't. I went across the street to the Gris-Gris Bar. I just didn't want to be alone."

The detective nodded. "Yeah, I'd imagine you might have been pretty scared being up there in that apartment by yourself after witnessing something like that downstairs."

Encouraged that he understood, Piper continued. "I was. And when I went to the bar, I had a couple drinks."

The detective waited.

"And talked too much," she blurted. "I told everyone who was standing around listening exactly what I'd seen. Then, last night, I was listening to *The Aaron Kane Show,* and I heard him talking about everything he'd heard me say. The whole radio audience heard it."

There. She had said it.

Confession always felt good.

PIPER LEFT THE POLICE STATION hoping that the detective had believed her when she told him that the last thing she would ever want to do was impede a police investigation. She made sure to mention that her father was a retired cop and her boyfriend was an FBI agent.

That never hurt.

She'd summoned up the courage to ask the detective a question before she left. "Do you have any leads in the murders?"

He'd answered the way she should have anticipated. "You know I can't tell you that, but I will tell you that we already knew you were the one that Aaron Kane was talking about on his show last night."

CHAPTER

78

Putting down the tiny paintbrush, Aaron sat back, clasped his hands over his round stomach, and beheld the result of all his hard work. The model of the *Natchez* had turned out wonderfully well. The pilothouse, the smokestacks, the huge American flag, the giant red paddlewheel at the rear, and dozens and dozens of tiny balusters circling the vessel's three floors. Each one of those annoying spindles had to be painted individually.

But now the splendor of the thing was worth all the effort. It was one of the prettiest models he'd ever built. Yet Aaron had decided against displaying it with all his other miniature vessels.

He was still shaken at the memory of the detectives waiting for him when he came out of the radio studio the night before. First they wanted to know who the woman was who had revealed the details of Bertrand Olivier's murder scene. Aaron had hesitated and gone through the motions of protesting that he wasn't going to give up a source. But when the detectives pressed, accusing him of obstructing a homicide investigation and berating him for stirring irrational fear in his listening audience, Aaron gave up Piper Donovan's name.

His respect for the New Orleans police had risen at the speed at which they responded to the information they'd picked up on his show. It demonstrated they could be efficient and sharp when they wanted to be. It also indicated that they were taking the murders on Royal Street very seriously.

The idea of touting the Hoodoo Killer had seemed like such a good idea. The increasing ratings showed that his plan was working. Aaron knew he could still get more mileage from the concept. But he also knew that the homicide detectives weren't fooling around. He had to be careful.

Aaron had planned to keep the model for himself, but now he had another thought. He would give the boat to Sabrina and Leo at their wedding celebration on the *Natchez* tomorrow night. Maybe the gesture of generosity would give him good juju with the spirits and keep his scheme working.

CHAPTER

79

APPROACHING THE BAKERY, Piper spotted a man with his hands cupped against the front window. She assumed he was only curious, wanting to see what he could of a murder scene. She was surprised when he stated the reason he was there.

"I'm here for the St. Joseph's bread. I buy it every year."

Piper had entirely forgotten the feast day.

"The bakery is closed for a while," she said. If the guy hadn't heard about the murder on the news, she didn't feel as though she should be the one to tell him. She didn't want to answer the inevitable questions that would follow. She'd learned her lesson about talking too much.

KNEADING A SMALL AMOUNT OF fondant until it was smooth and pliable, Piper used a light dusting of powdered sugar to keep it from sticking to the worktable. She tinted portions of the fondant in colors that would reflect the bride and groom—red for Sabrina's long hair, black for Leo's. She mixed the tiniest bit of orange to make a peach shade for their skin tones.

Piper took the flesh-colored fondant and divided it into portions for body parts. She made small balls for the heads and long, thicker logs for the torsos. Then she rolled the small arms and legs.

Assembling all the pieces to form the figures, Piper brushed a bit of water at each joint to make things hold together. She took care fashioning a simple A-line wedding dress and a veil along with a white chef's jacket.

Finally she tackled the facial features, using a very fine pastry brush to paint eyes, eyelashes, and mouths on the fondant faces. Satisfied with her whimsical wedding-couple creation, she took a picture with her iPhone and sent it to herself. Then she went into the office, turned on the computer there, entered her e-mail account, and printed out the picture. She was pleased enough with the image that she thought Marguerite might like it included in the bakery scrapbook.

Taking the book from the shelf, Piper flipped through the pages. She taped her picture onto a clean page near the back. Before she closed the scrapbook, she sat at the desk and browsed through it.

Bertrand really had been an artist, Piper thought sadly as she looked at the glorious images. The cakes he had created for special occasions were fabulous. Delicate christening cakes, festive

Christmas cakes, sumptuous anniversary cakes, and extravagant wedding cakes, all expertly decorated with a sure hand and an unfailing eye for detail. Piper cringed when she came to the picture of a rainbow-colored, three-dimensional marzipan snake cake that Bertrand had done for a child's birthday party.

Though Marguerite said she wanted to go on with the business, Piper wondered how she would manage without Bertrand. She supposed the designs could be copied by other skilled bakers, but the creativity and flair Bertrand possessed would not be easily duplicated. From what Piper had witnessed so far, Marguerite seemed confident and determined she could carry on. More power to her.

Leaving the cake section of the album, Piper started looking at the theme cookies. She grabbed a pencil and started to take some notes. She really wanted her mother to try these at The Icing on the Cupcake when Piper got home.

The jazz-instrument cookies were great, but she suspected they were far more popular in New Orleans than they would be in New Jersey. The same went for the voodoo dolls. The nursery-rhyme cookies were another story. Piper knew they would be a big hit in the child-driven, suburban world where she lived. She grabbed a pen from the cup on the desk and began sketching some of Bertrand's designs, knowing that she would add her own touches when she made them and, perhaps, create some others.

Jack and Jill, Little Miss Muffet sitting on her tuffet, Humpty Dumpty, the three little kittens who lost their mittens, Old King Cole, the mouse and the clock from "Hickory Dickory Dock," the three men in the tub.

Piper found herself reciting the rhyme in her mind.

Rub-a-dub-dub,
Three men in a tub,
And who do you think they be?
The butcher, the baker, the candlestick maker,
All put out to sea.

Rub-a-dub-dub. Wub-a-dub. Wub-a-dub. Piper thought of Connor, the bar owner's little boy, happily babbling in his playpen.

The butcher, the baker, the candlestick maker.

As she looked at the little mustachioed man with the baker's cap in the cookie boat, Piper was reminded of Bertrand. When he had created these charming cookie treasures, he could never have imagined what was coming his way.

The butcher, the baker, the candlestick maker.

Piper sat up straighter as she thought of it. Muffuletta Mike would be considered a butcher; working with meat was his profession. Bertrand was certainly a baker. Both of them had been murdered.

But what about the candlestick maker? Could that possibly be a future murder victim?

She tried to dismiss the notion as ridiculous. After all, the murder scenes had dripped with voodoo or hoodoo elements. But what if there was something else afoot? Something more. What if the nursery rhyme was the reason the victims had been chosen? If that was the case, someone else could be in danger.

Piper thought about the brass candlesticks she had won in the tricky-tray raffle. They sat alongside the silver ones that had already been in the apartment when she arrived. Both sets had come from the shop where Sabrina worked. Duchamps Antiques and Illuminations on Royal Street.

Maybe she was all wrong. But maybe she wasn't.

PIPER DEBATED WITH HERSELF. SHOULD she call Jack and tell him about her theory? She decided against it, knowing that he would only berate her for playing detective and sticking her nose where it didn't belong. She doubted, too, that the police would welcome her involvement.

Still, she didn't feel right about doing nothing.

It wouldn't hurt to warn the candlestick maker herself, would it?

AFTER LOOSELY COVERING THE RED velvet cake's layers with clean linen cloths, Piper washed her hands and grabbed her bag. Rather than exit through the back and have to walk all the way around the block to get to Royal Street, she summoned up the courage to walk through the hallway to the front of the bakery. She shivered as she passed the dumbwaiter.

Both the hall and the display area were covered with the black fingerprint-powder smudges.

Marguerite probably should hire a professional to really get the place sparkling again, thought Piper as she set the alarm and let herself out of the shop.

It was a gorgeous afternoon. The sun shone brightly, and it was a bit cooler than it had been. Piper detected a faint breeze as she watched happy tourists sauntering down the sidewalks.

Crossing the street, Piper approached Duchamps Antiques and Illuminations. The bell above the door tinkled as she entered. She expected the proprietor to greet her. But no one was in the front of the shop.

Walking in farther, Piper stopped at the sound of raised voices coming from the back room. The heated conversation apparently had been loud enough that the speakers hadn't heard the bell.

"It's too late, Falkner!" a woman yelled. "I signed the new will this morning."

"Well, change it back, Aunt Ellinore. What you're doing isn't fair. The Duchamps money should stay in the family."

Feeling embarrassed to be eavesdropping on a very personal conversation, Piper turned and left the shop. She could come back later.

CHAPTER

80

*T*he first order of business was to unobtrusively lock the front door. That way they would not be interrupted.

Ellinore was busying herself with straightening the beautiful objects on an old hutch near the rear of the shop. Her body was turned away. Now was the time. Now!

Quickly, silently, sneaking closer, carrying the bag full of living, breathing hoodoo clues.

A heavy candlestick was grabbed along the way. The elegant weapon came down hard against the back of Ellinore's skull with a sickening thud.

The woman gasped with surprise and pain as she collapsed, reaching out while falling forward and pulling over a carved mahogany side table with her. The crystal bowls and pitchers that *had been displayed on top slid and crashed to the floor, splintering into countless glittering fragments.*

As she lay amid the broken glass, Ellinore's eyes were closed, but a low, hoarse groan issued from deep in her throat. She wasn't dead yet.

It was dangerous to leave her on the shop floor. Though the door was locked and they were in the back, somebody just might be able to catch a glimpse of something from the front window. Better to finish the job where nobody could see.

Dragging Ellinore's limp figure through the crystal shards was no easy task. Her body was thick and heavy. Blood oozed from her head, and the bits of broken crystal pierced her skin in places, causing a red, sticky mess.

The door to the cellar was reached, and with one long, forceful heave, Ellinore was propelled down the hard, steep stairs. Her head smashed against the steps again and again as her body flipped over and over. Finally she lay motionless on the cold cement floor.

A quick check confirmed that she wasn't breathing. It was done now.

All that was left was to release the butterflies.

CHAPTER

81

PIPER PLAYED WITH the arrangement for the cake topper. She wasn't satisfied as she looked at the miniature paddleboat she'd purchased at the gift shop. The painted metal of the little vessel was cheerful and colorful, but it didn't look right sitting in between the fondant bride and groom. She decided to dip the paddleboat in chocolate.

As she melted the white pellets in a gleaming copper pot, Piper reminded herself to be sure to let Sabrina and Leo know that the steamboat was not to be eaten. It wouldn't be good to start out married life with a cracked tooth.

While she stirred the molten white chocolate, Piper glanced at her watch. It was a quarter to five. She wanted to get back over to the antique shop before it closed.

The paddleboat could wait. She turned off the stove and hurried out of the bakery.

A SMALL CROWD GATHERED IN front of Duchamps Antiques and Illuminations. They were staring through the front window, seemingly mesmerized by what they were watching inside. As Piper got closer, she could see why.

Dozens of sparkling chandeliers, all fully lit, hung from the showroom ceiling. Among them flitted scores of butterflies, their colorful wings flapping gracefully. The overall effect was breathtaking.

Was it some sort of marketing ploy, designed to lure people into the shop? If so, it didn't seem to be working. The onlookers seemed content just to stand on the sidewalk out front and watch the magical display inside.

Taking a deep breath, Piper decided to venture in. She excused herself as she made her way through the group. Opening the front door, she entered quickly, trying hard not to let any of the butterflies escape.

"Hello?" she called. She batted the swarm of butterflies that enveloped her as she walked into the shop.

No one responded to her call.

A butterfly alighted on her sleeve as Piper went deeper into the shop.

She called out again. "Hello? Anybody here?"

Piper winced as the flying insects tangled themselves in her hair. Butterflies flapped, around and around. But she could detect no other movement. Her pulse began to race.

She remembered what she had heard Cecil, the musician, say on Aaron Kane's radio show. The butterfly was the symbol of the voodoo loa associated with St. Joseph. Oh, no! Had she gotten here too late?

Her instinct was to turn, run, and get help. But still Piper kept on going. Maybe she was wrong and alerting the police would just be foolish. Or maybe Ellinore Duchamps was still alive and needed help. Either way Piper had to see what the situation was before doing anything else.

The overturned table and shards of sparkling crystal confirmed some sort of accident. The smeared dark trail of blood confirmed something much worse. Piper followed the path that led to the closed cellar door.

She hesitated before opening it. Now she *knew* she should get the police. But what if Ellinore was down there, alive and needing help? What if Piper's immediate attention could save a life?

Yet what if a killer was also down there . . . waiting?

SHE CALLED 911, QUICKLY GIVING her name, where she was, and a brief summary of the situation. The dispatcher instructed her to leave the antique shop immediately and wait outside for the police to arrive. Reluctantly, Piper complied.

As she waited on the sidewalk, she thought of Falkner and

the snatch of angry conversation she'd overheard in the shop earlier that afternoon. Had the verbal fight turned into a physical confrontation?

A patrolman arrived on foot. Piper saw him rest his hand on his holstered gun as he entered the shop. Immediately after, a squad car pulled to the curb. Two more officers got out, one going inside, the other instructing the burgeoning crowd out front to move back.

The minutes ticked by. More cars arrived, followed by an ambulance. The crowd was at its largest and a TV news crew appeared when the stretcher bearing the body bag filled with Ellinore's remains was wheeled out of the building.

THE POLICE WERE CANVASSING THE crowd, looking for witnesses who might have seen anything that could help with the investigation of the third murder on Royal Street in less than a week. Piper approached a familiar detective, the one she'd spoken with at the police station just that morning.

"Ah, Miss Donovan," he said when he saw her. "I hear you're the one that called this in. You sure do get around, don't you?"

Piper squirmed uncomfortably.

"What were you doing here?" asked the detective. "You don't look to me like the type who goes in for antiques."

"I came over to warn the owner," said Piper.

"Warn her about what?" asked the detective suspiciously.

"That she could be in danger."

"How's that?"

Piper explained that she'd been working in the bakery, looking at some designs of nursery-rhyme cookies, when she came upon the three-men-in-a-tub cookie and realized that the first murders on Royal Street had been those of a butcher and a baker.

"So I thought that the next murder victim could be a candlestick maker. I thought I should warn the owner."

Even as she said it, Piper knew how outlandish it sounded.

She caught the detective rolling his eyes slightly. "All right," he said. "Let's continue. Did you see anyone when you arrived inside the shop?"

"No," said Piper uncertainly. "Not really."

"What does that mean? Did you or didn't you?"

Piper hesitated. Falkner had been kind to her the night Bertrand was killed. She didn't want to implicate him in a murder. Yet he *had* been in the shop, arguing with Ellinore Duchamps just a few hours ago. Piper had to tell the police. To withhold the information would be unconscionable.

She described what she'd overheard. The detective scribbled some notes, shaking his head while he did so.

"I forgot to ask you this morning, Miss Donovan. When did you get to town?"

"Last Thursday."

The detective nodded. "So you've been here for all three of the Royal Street murders."

Piper's eyes widened. Had he thought she was casting suspicion on Falkner as a way to cover her own guilt?

"Are you looking at me as a suspect?" she asked incredulously.

"We're looking at everybody," said the detective. He closed his notebook. "All right, you can go for now. But I have to ask you not to leave New Orleans."

Piper was stunned as she turned to cross the street. She'd been on the scene of two murders in the last two days. The cops could easily consider the possibility that she was reporting the crimes as a way to shift suspicion away from herself. But then it occurred to her that she had her own question to ask. She had to know the answer. She went back and found the detective.

"Would it have made any difference," she asked earnestly, "if I went right downstairs without calling the police? Could I have helped her?"

The detective frowned. "I'm afraid not, Miss Donovan. The body was already cold. It looks like she'd been dead for a while."

CHAPTER

82

GOOD NEWS TRAVELED FAST.

Jack listened, brow furrowed, as his FBI colleague in New Orleans described the latest murder in the French Quarter. Jack slammed his fist on the desk when he heard that Piper was the one who had made the 911 call to the police.

Barely anyone looked up from the other desks in the New York squad room. They were used to Jack's temper. Though he preferred to call it passion.

At first Jack was furious at the thought of the NOPD putting a tail on Piper. She was no more a murderer than the man in the moon. But the more he thought about it, Jack decided against calling and putting in a good word for her with the cops down there.

Let them keep her under police surveillance. At least she'd be safe.

"All right, thanks, Louie," said Jack resignedly. "Keep me posted, willya, buddy?"

When he hung up the phone, Jack wanted to call Piper and make sure she was all right. Yet he didn't. Maybe she had to really be left on her own for now. Maybe then she would finally learn her lesson. She was an actress and a cake designer, *not* a law-enforcement officer.

He thought, *Sometimes the best love is tough love.*

CHAPTER

83

IN SPITE OF the latest murder, or maybe because of it, business was brisk that night at the Gris-Gris Bar. The customers were buzzing with conversations about the murder next door and the butterflies let loose in the antique shop. Even those who'd been skeptical about the Hoodoo Killer before were now convinced.

Falkner's face was ashen as he entered the bar. He slowly climbed up onto a stool at the counter and ordered a stiff drink.

"I'm sorry about your aunt, Falkner," said the bartender. "You look like you've lost your best friend."

"Hardly," said Falkner, sighing deeply. "She totally screwed me, Wuzzy. She changed her will before she died. I'm out."

"Ouch! That hurts, bro."

"And you want to know the best part?" asked Falkner. He took a long swallow of bourbon before answering his own question. "The cops knocked on my door to question *me*. Seems somebody came into the antique shop this afternoon and heard me and Ellinore arguing."

Wuzzy waited for more.

"I asked them to think about it, Wuz. Why would I want to kill Ellinore? I had nothing to gain. I was already written out of her will."

"What did they say to that?" asked Wuzzy.

"The detective said I could have killed her in a fit of rage. Then he started asking me questions about my connections to Muffuletta Mike and Bertrand Olivier."

Wuzzy's jaw dropped. "Falkner, I think you better get a lawyer, bro."

Falkner laid his head down on the bar and closed his eyes. A minute later he raised it again and looked at the bartender.

"It's ghoulish, Wuzzy. But at least something good will come from my aunt's death. Now *you* can get her shop and expand the bar."

84

PIPER BRACED HERSELF for the call to her parents. She didn't want them to hear the news on television. She hoped to reassure them that although she was shaken, she was all right. Both her mother and father got on the extensions to listen to her story.

"Enough is enough, Piper," said Vin when she finished. "You've got to come home. Now."

"I can't, Dad. Even if I wanted to, I can't leave now."

"That's nonsense," said her mother. "Why not?"

Piper hesitated.

"Why not?" Vin pressed.

"Because the police told me I shouldn't leave New Orleans."

"Dear God, Piper!" cried Terri. "They don't think you're a suspect, do they?"

"I don't know *what* they think," said Piper. "But *I* don't think it would be a smart move to take off now. It would make me look guilty, like I have something to hide."

"Piper's right, Terri," said Vin. "She's got to stick around down there for now. But damn it, Piper, you've got to promise me to just do what you went down there to do. Stay at the bakery, make your cakes, and don't get into any more trouble."

"I promise, Dad," said Piper. "Believe me, I totally promise."

Determined to keep her vow, Piper washed up, took a Tylenol PM, and got into bed. But she couldn't keep herself from tuning in to *The Aaron Kane Show*. She turned on the radio and listened in the dark.

Caller after caller chimed in with observations about the latest murder on Royal Street. The butterflies flitting around the crime scene had captured everyone's attention. Some of the regular listeners applauded the host for calling it from the first.

"Your guest on last night's show nailed it, Aaron. It was as if that street musician could see the future when he talked about Loko, the voodoo loa, being associated with St. Joseph's Day and telling us that Loko shows himself as a butterfly."

"Keep up the good work, Aaron. You were way ahead of the curve. You got onto this hoodoo thing last week when it was only Muffeletta Mike who'd been killed. Now there are two more victims. Kudos to you, sir."

"I agree with the previous caller, Aaron. You are either

clairvoyant or the luckiest man alive to have declared a hoodoo murderer so soon. But it looks like you sure were right. It makes my skin crawl just thinking about it."

Aaron chuckled. "Well, I know I'm not clairvoyant—although I *may* just be the luckiest man alive. But I think the questions we have to ask ourselves tonight are these: What are the New Orleans police doing to protect us? Are they just waiting around for a fourth victim? What's being done to make sure the Hoodoo Killer doesn't strike again?"

THURSDAY
MARCH 20

CHAPTER

85

IT WAS SABRINA'S fourth trip in twenty-four hours to Louis Armstrong New Orleans International Airport, greeting and shuttling newly arrived wedding guests to the Windsor Court Hotel just outside the French Quarter.

The baggage claim area was already busy as the bride waited anxiously for her mother to arrive. The early-morning flight from Washington, D.C., had landed on time. Sabrina craned her neck to catch a glimpse of her mother coming into view.

Mother and daughter embraced in a long, firm hug. When they pulled back from each other, Sabrina's mother immediately noticed her daughter's red-rimmed eyes.

"What's wrong, sweetheart?" she asked. "You've been crying."

"Oh, Mama, I'm so glad you're here. But let's not go into it all now. We'll get your bag, and we can talk later. I thought we could go to Court of Two Sisters for the Jazz Brunch Buffet."

"Sounds perfect."

Forty-five minutes later, mother and daughter sat in the wisteria-covered brick courtyard of the historic French Quarter restaurant as a jazz trio serenaded them and the other customers. After ordering mimosas they went to the extensive buffet, where they helped themselves to made-to-order seafood omelets, sausage, grits, and grillades.

As errant wisteria petals floated gracefully down onto their table, Sabrina barely touched her food, but she quickly ordered another mimosa.

"Okay, Sabrina. Now. Tell me what's wrong."

"Well," Sabrina began. "I guess you've seen the stories on the news about the recent murders here, right?"

"As a matter of fact, I haven't, honey. Taking care of Grandma is a full-time job. I hardly know what's going on in the world anymore."

Sabrina reached over and patted her mother's hand. "I'm sorry, Mama. I know you have your hands full up there. I wish I lived closer and could help you."

"Don't worry about that now, Sabrina. Your life is here with Leo, and that's the way it should be. I should have been down here helping you with everything, but I just couldn't leave Grandma alone. As it was, I don't feel all that comfortable with the caretaker I found to look after her for these next few days."

"That's all right, Mama. Leo and I have had fun planning it ourselves. Until this last week, and then all sorts of horrible things began to happen. Now I wonder if we should have postponed the whole thing."

Sabrina described the gruesome events of the past week.

Her mother's eyes widened. "The murders were all right here on Royal Street?" she asked. "And they are all tied to voodoo? Dear Lord!"

After taking another sip of her mimosa, Sabrina continued. "The worst part, for me at least, Mama, is that the third victim was my boss. She was killed yesterday."

"Ellinore? The woman who's been so nice to you? The one who gave you that chandelier you love as a wedding gift?"

Sabrina nodded.

"Oh, I'm so sorry, sweetheart! Why didn't you call me?"

"I didn't want to worry you right before you left. I knew you'd be here this morning. That seemed time enough to share the bad news." A tear seeped from the corner of Sabrina's eye, and she dabbed at it with her napkin. "Oh, Mama. I never thought that this was the way my wedding was going to turn out."

The older woman comforted the younger one throughout the rest of the meal. After they had finished eating and paid the check, Sabrina's mother took a handful of change from her wallet. She gave half the coins to her daughter.

"What are these for?" asked Sabrina.

Her mother pointed. "There's a fountain over there and a wishing well over there. Take your pick. Throw in the coins and make your wish. I will, too. Everything is going to work out, Sabrina. You'll see."

Sabrina smiled weakly. "You always make me feel better, Mama. Thank you."

As she tossed the pennies, nickels, and dimes into the wishing well, Sabrina prayed that her mother was right.

CHAPTER

86

Piper lined up the round red velvet cakes, from large to small, on the bakery worktable. Though the tops of each appeared to be flat, just slightly uneven layers could add up to a wedding cake with a pronounced slope. She found a long serrated knife in a drawer and gently sliced away any high spots. Next Piper torted the cakes, splitting each horizontally to form two equal halves.

Flour. That was the unlikely ingredient in her mother's favorite frosting. Piper whisked it into milk in a saucepan, stirring constantly until it thickened. When the mixture was the consistency of a dense cake batter, Piper took it off the stove and added some vanilla.

While waiting for the frosting base to cool, she creamed together butter and sugar until the result was light and fluffy. Then she added it to the completely cooled mixture of milk, flour, and vanilla. Beating, beating, beating it all together until it resembled whipped cream.

Piper stuck a spoon into the finished frosting and sampled it, closing her eyes and purring at the amazing taste. As many times as her mother made it, Piper never failed to relish the flavor. If and when she got married, this would certainly be the frosting on her wedding cake!

Turning back to the cake, she selected an appropriately sized cardboard round for the bottom of the layers. Each tier had to be frosted individually before the entire cake could be stacked and assembled. The bottom layer of the cake was not strong enough to support the weight of the other cakes on top of it without getting squashed. Piper strategically inserted wooden dowels into the cake base before placing the next tier.

She stood back to take a look at her creation thus far. The tiers were even, glimmering with snowy white icing. But she had to decide how to decorate the sides. Bertrand and Piper had never come to an agreement on that. He hadn't wanted to go with her idea of using the fleur-de-lis, the symbol of New Orleans. It was too much of a cliché, he thought.

Piper went into the office, turned on the computer, and clicked on Google. She started typing "NEW ORLEANS WEDDING," and after the first few letters a list of the most recent searches beginning with "NEW" dropped down from the input box. "NEW ORLEANS ST. PATRICK'S DAY" was at the top.

Piper finished typing in the rest of her search and, hitting the ENTER key, came across several entries that described baking the wedding cake with ribbons coming out of the sides. To each ribbon was attached a silver charm. Before the cake was cut, the bride would call female guests up to pull out the ribbons. Each charm had a meaning and foretold the future. A ring meant "next to marry." A thimble or a button meant "old maid." A horseshoe or a four-leaf clover was good luck. A heart meant that true love was in the offing.

What an awesome tradition! Piper wished she had come across it sooner. But she could still pay homage to the custom in a small way.

She went back to the kitchen, filled a piping bag with icing, and began to fashion swirling ribbons on the side of the cake. She had finished and was flanking the chocolate-covered paddleboat with the fondant bride and groom for the top of the cake when the phone rang. Marguerite was calling.

"I wanted to see how you're holding up, Piper."

"How am *I* holding up? What about *you,* Marguerite?"

"I'm all right," said Marguerite. "I'm so busy I guess it all hasn't hit me. But I don't like to think of you by yourself over there. With a third murder, you must be so shaken."

"I'm not gonna lie. It's hard to take it all in, but I'm just about done with the big cake," Piper replied. "I'm trying to focus on that."

"Take a picture and send it to me, will you?" asked Marguerite. "I'm not going to be able to come into the bakery or go to the party on the *Natchez* tonight. I'm just not up to it."

"Of course. I completely understand, Marguerite."

Piper *did* understand, but she was still a bit disappointed. A photograph was fine, but actually seeing the wedding cake was much better. She was proud of what she had created, and she wanted another professional to admire it. Still, Piper was well aware that Marguerite had more on her mind than wedding cakes. Marguerite needed to take care of herself and get some rest if she could.

"The delivery van will be there at four o'clock to pick up the cake and transport it to the *Natchez*," said Marguerite. "And you'll go over there later and make sure that everything is set up correctly?"

"Definitely," said Piper. "Don't worry about a thing."

When she hung up, Piper took a picture of the cake and sent it to Marguerite.

THE REST OF THE AFTERNOON passed quickly as Piper prepared the first stage of the bananas Foster cake for the smaller party the following night at Bistro Sabrina. One layer of moist, rum-soaked cake would be covered with thick caramel sauce, and the other three would have cream-cheese frosting.

As she mashed ripe bananas for the cake batter, Piper tried to keep her mind on the task at hand, but she couldn't help thinking about Ellinore Duchamps's murder. Perhaps if Piper had gotten there earlier to warn the woman, Ellinore would still be alive. Guilt was another item to put on her mental list of things to discuss with a therapist when she got back home.

But she comforted herself somewhat with the knowledge that when she'd mentioned the butcher–baker–candlestick maker theory to the detective, he hadn't seemed to think the idea held any water.

Tired and ready for a hot shower, Piper climbed the outdoor stairs to her apartment. She hoped she might be able to squeeze in a short nap before dressing and heading over to the *Natchez*.

She opened the French doors to the balcony and felt a warm breeze waft in. The fresh air felt good to her after she'd been cooped up inside the bakery all day. She stepped out to enjoy the warmth of the late-afternoon sun as she looked down on Royal Street. She averted her eyes from the yellow police tape draped around the latest crime scene.

She started to do some of her yoga stretching exercises to work out the tightness in her neck and shoulders. Then she closed her eyes and breathed deeply, in and out. She felt better.

As she turned to go back inside to take her shower, Piper looked down at the street one more time. She noticed a man leaning against a streetlamp. She was sure he was looking up at her, watching.

CHAPTER

87

THE MUDDY WATERS of the Mississippi River flowed beneath Sabrina and Leo's friends and family gathered for cocktails on the upper deck of the giant paddleboat. The breeze blew more heavily out on the water, causing dresses to flutter and paper napkins to fly off the tables. Nobody seemed to mind. They were busy chatting, laughing, and enjoying the five-piece jazz band. Trumpet, clarinet, trombone, bass, and drum played smooth, happy songs: "Fly Me to the Moon," "All of Me," "Cheek to Cheek," "Walking My Baby Back Home."

Piper found herself humming as she took the stairs down to the lower deck. She asked a steward to point the way to the private dining room. She wanted to check on her work. When she entered the room, she saw that the groom had beat her to it.

"It looks great," said Leo as he stood grinning at the cake. "The chef's jacket on the little groom is a nice touch."

"Glad you like it," said Piper.

Leo offered his hand to her. "Thank you, Piper. With all that's been happening, it's a relief to have something come out right. I know that Sabrina will love it."

Piper shook back firmly. "I hope so, Leo. It was a pleasure to work on something for such a life-affirming occasion."

Leo looked at her intently. "You know, until just this minute I hadn't given any thought to how tough this past week must have been for you, Piper. Coming down here thinking you were going to be spending your time working with a renowned baker only to find yourself smack in the middle of a killing spree. The worst, discovering Bertrand's dead body. That must have been horrific."

"It was," said Piper softly. "I'm trying not to think about it."

"Of course you are," said Leo. "None of us should think about any of it tonight. Right?"

Piper smiled as Leo put a hand on her shoulder. "Right," she agreed.

"Tell me again," said Leo as he looked at the wedding cake one more time. "What kind of icing are you using on the cake for tomorrow night?"

"Cream cheese."

Leo shook his head. "You know, I'm sorry I didn't let you know earlier, but I've been so distracted by everything. I'm not a real cream-cheese fan. Too heavy. I think buttercream would be better. Maybe you can spice it up with some pecans or crumbled pralines or something. Would you mind doing that? It's not too late, is it?"

"Of course not, Leo," said Piper. "You should have exactly what you want on your wedding day."

Hoooooooo!

Piper winced at the deafening sound of the paddleboat's horn. The vessel was about to pull away from the Toulouse Street Dock. Piper stood at the railing as the strong breeze off the river whipped at the folds of her long skirt. She watched the lights of the New Orleans skyline glittering against the darkening sky as the *Natchez* began its cruise down the Mississippi. She took out her iPhone and snapped some pictures.

"Pretty, isn't it?"

She looked up to see Falkner Duchamps standing beside her. Piper pulled back with alarm, missing as she tried to slide the phone into her shoulder bag. She didn't hear its protective rubber covering hit the deck.

"What's wrong?" asked Falkner when he saw the wary expression on her face. "I thought we were friends."

"I'm surprised to see you," said Piper.

He frowned. "Oh, you mean because of my aunt's death?"

"Yes," said Piper. "I'm very sorry about that."

Falkner shrugged. "We weren't the closest."

"I gathered that," said Piper.

Falkner looked at her sharply. "What do you mean?"

Piper hesitated before answering. Should she tell him that she'd heard him yelling at Ellinore about changing her will? She decided to go ahead. A person was innocent until proven guilty. Falkner should know that the police were aware she'd overheard the fight.

She told him.

"So you're the one?" he asked incredulously. "You're the one who sent the cops banging on my door?"

Piper nodded.

"You shouldn't have done that, Piper!" Falkner yelled, his face reddening. He pounded his fist on the railing. "You should have come to me first and let me explain!"

"I had to tell the police what I heard," said Piper quietly. "They're investigating a murder spree. I had to tell the truth before somebody else ends up dead."

"Telling the truth can get people in a lot of trouble, Piper!" yelled Falkner as he stepped closer to her.

"Are you threatening me, Falkner?"

Before Falkner could answer, a man dressed in a navy blazer appeared beside them.

"Is this man bothering you, miss?" he asked.

Falkner quickly pivoted and stormed away. Piper turned to thank the man for coming to her aid, but he was already walking in the other direction. She had seen him just briefly, but his appearance struck a familiar chord.

Was he the same guy who'd been leaning against the lamppost watching her on the balcony this afternoon?

BEFORE DINNER BOTH THE BEST man and the maid of honor made toasts to the bride and groom. The assembled guests clapped and cheered, their enthusiasm and goodwill overshadowing, for a little while at least, all thoughts of murder. Everyone wanted Sabrina and Leo to be happy and enjoy their special evening.

After the buffet dinner of seafood gumbo, snow crab claws, oysters Bienville, crawfish étouffée, and creole jambalaya, Aaron stood at the front of the room enthusiastically clinking his water glass with a spoon. When the guests quieted down, he made a big show of presenting his wedding gift to Sabrina and Leo. The couple seemed thrilled with the model of the *Natchez*.

"Oh, it's wonderful, Aaron," said Sabrina, warmly embracing the portly man. "We'll find a special place for this and always remember you and this magical evening. Thank you so much."

Piper watched, thinking that Aaron clearly liked the fuss Sabrina made over him, as well as the guests coming over to shake his hand and clap him on the back afterward. She supposed that the radio personality really craved being the center of attention.

That "hoodoo murder" theme of his had probably fed his need to be noticed.

STRAINS OF "THAT OLD BLACK MAGIC" filled the air as the guests streamed off the paddleboat. Piper wished that Jack were with her, holding her hand as they walked down the gangplank together after the romantic dinner cruise. She decided she was going to give in and call him tonight when she got back to the apartment.

First, though, she had to stop at the bakery kitchen. If Leo wanted buttercream frosting with something extra added to it for tomorrow's cake, Piper wanted to have it all decided before she went to sleep, with the recipe printed out and waiting for her when she arrived at the bakery the next morning.

Some of the guests left the wharf and proceeded into the French Quarter to continue partying. Others went to cars in the wharf's parking lot. Piper joined the rest who stood at the corner hailing cabs. While she waited, she spotted the man in the navy blazer again.

As her taxi pulled away from the curb, Piper looked out the rear window. The man was still watching her. She shivered as they made eye contact.

CHAPTER

88

THE UNDERCOVER COP realized that he'd been made.

Piper Donovan knew that he was watching her. He was pretty sure that she'd spotted him as he stood looking up at her apartment balcony on Royal Street that afternoon. And now she had stared right at him as she drove away.

He cursed the fact that he'd intervened in the altercation between Piper and Falkner Duchamps on the boat that evening. But he had no choice. Duchamps was clearly intimidating Piper. Instinctively he'd felt he had to intervene.

It had all happened so quickly. He'd hoped that Piper had been too focused on Duchamps to pay close attention to the stranger who came to her aid. He'd tried to get away before she had a chance to thank him.

But now the worried expression on Piper's face, the directness of her gaze from the cab window confirmed that she was onto him. Perhaps she didn't realize that she was being tailed by the police. But she almost certainly understood that she was being watched by someone she didn't know. Against the backdrop of the eerie and gory multiple murders on Royal Street, that knowledge had to be deeply unnerving for Piper.

The thought crossed his mind that he should tell her who he was, so she'd realize that he wasn't a physical threat to her. He wasn't some crazy Hoodoo Killer out to make her his next victim. But telling her would defeat the whole point of the surveillance.

Now he pulled the collar of his blazer up against the cold breeze that came off the river. He didn't think that Piper Donovan was a ruthless murderer killing Royal Street merchants in her spare time. She certainly didn't fit any profile he could imagine. But the brass was putting on the heat and insisting that every possible lead be pursued. He had orders to follow. Until his shift was over, that's exactly what he was going to do.

CHAPTER

89

THE TAXI DROPPED Piper in front of Boulangerie Bertrand. She went in, turned off the alarm, and quickly switched on all the lights. Even then it was creepy being in the bakery at night, walking through the hallway where Bertrand was killed. Piper had considered asking the driver to take her to the back entrance, but going through the small trash-strewn alleyway wasn't a more attractive alternative. She was scared that there would be rats skulking around in the dark.

She hurried past the dumbwaiter and went directly to the small office. As she booted up the computer, she noticed a light blinking on the desk phone. She punched in the code and listened to the message.

"Hello, this is Simon Seaford from Consolidated Cuisine. I'm trying to reach Mrs. Bertrand Olivier. We've been dealing with her

*husband, Bertrand, and under these tragic circumstances we need
to speak with her. The home phone is unlisted, and, understandably,
there's been no answer on Bertrand's mobile. Please let Mrs. Olivier
know that we are trying to reach her. It's urgent."*

The caller left a phone number.

Piper debated with herself. It was after ten o'clock, and
Marguerite could already be asleep. Yet the man had insisted it was
an important matter. Picking up the phone again, she consulted
the phone list on the wall and called Marguerite at home.

When Marguerite answered sleepily, Piper apologized
profusely before passing on the message and the return number.

"How did it go on the *Natchez* tonight? Were Sabrina and
Leo satisfied with your cake?" asked Marguerite.

"They seemed to be," said Piper. "And I noticed that most of
the guests cleaned their plates. That's always a positive sign. So
many times you go to a wedding reception and people just take a
bite or two of the cake and leave the rest."

"Ah, good," said Marguerite. "Bertrand would be so pleased.
Thank you very much, Piper. I don't know what I'm going to do
without you when you go back north."

"I was happy to do it, Marguerite. Now there's just tomorrow's
cake to finish. That's why I'm in the office now. Leo told me
tonight he doesn't want cream-cheese icing on the bananas Foster
cake. I'm gonna Google around on the Internet for buttercream
recipes with a little something extra."

"It's so late, Piper," Marguerite said with alarm in her voice.
"Don't do that now. You can do it in the morning. You worked
hard today. Go upstairs and get some rest."

CHAPTER

90

IT WAS A cold but crystal-clear night in Manhattan. Jack stood at the window of his apartment in Peter Cooper Village. When he positioned himself at precisely the right angle, he could see the top of the Empire State Building glowing white against the midnight blue sky.

He wished Piper were with him.

Both of them were stubborn. Neither had called the other. Jack had vowed to himself that he wasn't going to be the one to give in.

He sighed heavily and walked over to the small bar in the corner of the living room. Pouring some scotch into a glass, he could feel his resolve weakening. He was tired of the game they were playing now, waiting to see who would break down and call. There was little doubt that eventually they would get over their disagreement. What did it matter who made the first move? Was he just being a macho jerk, trying to show her who was boss? Jack didn't like to think about himself that way.

He loved Piper. Pure and simple. He wanted to hear her voice.

Jack put down his glass and picked up the phone. But Piper didn't pick up as it rang and rang, finally going into voice mail. He didn't leave a message.

CHAPTER

91

PIPER WANTED TO speak with Jack. She checked the office clock. It was getting late. If she was going to call, she shouldn't wait any longer. She wouldn't want to wake him.

She was about to pick up the receiver on the desk phone again when she realized she didn't even have Jack's number committed to memory. She was so dependent now on her iPhone that she made her calls from her contacts list rather than entering numbers. Besides, it was better to make a personal call on her own phone anyway. She rummaged through her bag looking for the phone.

Where was it? She couldn't find it.

Dumping the contents of the bag on the desk, she sorted through lipsticks, mascara, blush, tissues, a brush, notebooks, receipts, a wallet, keys, pens, and pencils. She felt increasingly distressed.

Where could it be?

She looked around the office and kitchen. Then she traced her steps back through the hallway to the salesroom, glancing in every direction as she searched. Opening the front door, Piper checked the sidewalk in front of the bakery and walked along the curb for several yards one way and then the other. Perhaps the phone had fallen in the street when she got out of the taxi and been kicked aside by a pedestrian or hit by the cab's rear tire as it drove away.

Nothing.

She told herself to calm down and try to remember when she'd last had it. She was sure she hadn't used it in the taxi. The last time she could recall having it was when she'd taken pictures on the paddleboat. She'd put the phone back into her purse when Falkner approached her.

Piper returned to the office and called directory assistance for the number of the *Natchez*. When she called it, she got a recorded message with an announcement of the operating hours. She'd have to call again in the morning.

There was no way she was going to be able to go upstairs and fall right asleep now. She was too wound up. Sighing with resignation, Piper decided she might as well go ahead and figure out that frosting recipe. Beginning with Leo's suggestion of making a buttercream frosting mixed with crumbled pralines, Piper typed the first few letters into the Google search engine.

"B-U-T-T-E-R."

Instantly a list of the most recently searched terms, beginning with those letters, dropped down from the input box. Piper's eyes shifted upward and glanced at it. She immediately felt a tingle shoot through her system as she noticed the search at the top of the list.

"BUTTERFLY RELEASE."

CHAPTER

92

Traffic was relatively light on the streets that led from the Garden District to the French Quarter. Marguerite drove along St. Charles Avenue, where the green streetcars had ceased running for the night. Even in the darkness, she could see the silhouettes of the Greek Revival, Italianate, and Queen Anne–style mansions along the road framed by massive, ancient live oaks.

She tried to remain calm. The call to the buyers that Bertrand had lined up could wait until tomorrow. The trip to the bakery could not.

The minute Piper had mentioned that she was going to use the office computer for a recipe search, Marguerite felt a rush of adrenaline. How stupid she felt! With all her extensive planning, she had forgotten one crucial thing: All the research she'd done to map out her murder spree was sitting, for any and all to see, right there on her computer.

The World Wide Web had provided her whatever information she needed on voodoo and hoodoo, the symbols of the loas and the offerings they preferred. Various Web sites had pointed the way to where she could buy snakes and order butterflies. And the computer she used could document every keystroke she'd made. Anyone seeing her search history could piece together every step she'd taken to implement her deadly scheme. Living in the computer age had made murder easy.

The computer couldn't take credit, though, for the plan itself. That was all Marguerite's idea and, now, she was marveling at the cleverness of it.

After years of excruciating hurt and humiliation at the knowledge of Bertrand's disgusting womanizing, Marguerite had had enough. The pain she'd suffered, pretending she didn't notice each time he devoured attractive women with his eyes or touched them in whatever way he could. Bertrand thought she was oblivious to his using the upstairs apartment for his trysts. But his travels in the dumbwaiter, sneaking in and watching unsuspecting female guests, bothered Marguerite the most.

She still cringed when she thought of the most mortifying event of all. Last year her very own sister had come to visit and awoke in the middle of the night to find Bertrand standing by her bed leering down at her. Candice had been scared to death at first and thoroughly disgusted later. Bertrand had given some lame excuse about wanting to check if a recently installed air-conditioning system was working well up there. Marguerite's sister left the next morning, but not before she pulled Marguerite aside and urged her to divorce her lecherous husband.

But for Marguerite divorce was not an option. She wasn't going to settle for half of what they'd built. She deserved it all. The Consolidated Cuisine acquisition was about to go through with the plan of opening Boulangerie Bertrand franchises around the country. She'd be truly rich.

"Pig!" Marguerite spat as the car reached Canal Street.

That's what Bertrand was. He was cocky, too. When he got out of bed that night after the dinner at Bistro Sabrina, Marguerite suspected he might be going back to the French Quarter to sneak in and watch the latest pretty female he'd lured to New Orleans. There had been many qualified applicants for the guest-baker position, but Marguerite was sure Bertrand chose Piper Donovan after he saw her picture online.

That night there was no point in confronting Bertrand. She was way past that. Marguerite had already decided what she was going to do about him weeks ago. The first phase of her plan was scheduled to begin just a few hours later.

She wanted Bertrand dead, yet she didn't want to be a suspect. Marguerite knew that the police always looked at family members first in their homicide investigations. But if she killed Bertrand in the middle of a murder *spree*, the cops wouldn't look her way.

The idea for the other victims came to her one day as she worked beside Bertrand in the bakery.

He was decorating nursery-rhyme cookies. As she watched him piping a tiny mustache on the middle figure of the three characters in a little cookie boat, she decided who else would die. The rhyme itself suggested them.

The baker would be in the middle: Bertrand. So there'd have to be a butcher and a candlestick maker to complete the rhyme: Muffuletta Mike and Ellinore Duchamps. Though neither of them had wronged her, Marguerite didn't care. It worked out well for her plan that they all made their living on Royal Street.

To keep the police even farther away, Marguerite had decided to make all three murders look as though they were parts of voodoo rituals. The usual motives for murder wouldn't even be considered. Investigators would be distracted by voodoo clues.

But if they decided to check her computer, the police would be able to trace her electronic steps and figure out what she had done.

She had to get the computer.

On Royal Street the lights were on inside Boulangerie Bertrand. Piper hadn't closed the shop and gone upstairs after all. Why hadn't she done as she was told?

Marguerite was seized with panic.

Fear quickly changed to resolve. If a fourth murder were necessary, so be it. While she had no desire to kill Piper, she would if she had to. Marguerite would be able to tell right away by the expression on Piper's face, by the look of terror in her eyes, whether the young woman had uncovered the secrets in the computer. Piper couldn't possibly be a good enough actress to conceal the horror of that discovery.

Marguerite drove down to the corner and turned, steering the car into the narrow passage behind the bakery. Alleys were scarce in the French Quarter, with shops, cafés, and hotels built on top of one another, side by side and back to back. Tonight Marguerite was especially grateful that Boulangerie Bertrand had that rarest of amenities in the center of New Orleans: a back alley.

That advantage had tipped the scales when she and Bertrand chose the building for their business. Deliveries could be made to the rear door rather than having big sacks of flour, sugar, and other supplies hauled through the front. At the time Marguerite had never dreamed that the passageway would facilitate anything more than that.

Tonight the alley was going to help her get away with murder.

CHAPTER

93

PIPER TAPPED IN just the first two letters of every term she could think of that related to the murders.

"D-A." Up came "DAMBALLAH" at the very top of the recent-searches menu.

"L-O." Up came "LOKO."

"S-N"—"SNAKES."

Leaning back in her chair, Piper was shocked and in disbelief. Maybe she was overreacting. There had to be another explanation. The one that was running through her mind was too horrible to be real.

Only Bertrand and Marguerite used the computer. Bertrand was dead. That left Marguerite. Had she killed her husband? Had Marguerite killed Muffuletta Mike and Ellinore Duchamps as well?

Should she call the police? Maybe she was wrong about Marguerite. But shouldn't the police be informed of what Piper had come across on the computer? She was determined to follow Jack's and her father's advice and let the pros figure it out.

As Piper reached for the telephone, she heard the back door to the kitchen open. She turned to see Marguerite standing behind her. Piper tried but failed to keep the fear from her facial expression.

"Put down that phone," commanded Marguerite. "Now."

CHAPTER

94

JACK CLICKED THE remote control, and the TV screen went black. He got up from the couch and turned off the lamps, then walked down the hall to the bedroom. Before he went to sleep, he wanted to try Piper again.

As he undressed, Jack found comfort in the thought that Piper was going to be home this weekend. When they were together again, things would be all right between them. He hated when she went off and he couldn't be sure whether or not she was safe. Still, he didn't want to be some Neanderthal who resented his woman for doing her own thing.

Getting into bed, Jack called Piper's cell phone once more. It rang three times before a man's voice answered.

"Who's this?" Jack asked warily.

"Leo Yancy. Who's this?"

"I'm trying to reach Piper Donovan. This is her friend, Jack Lombardi."

"Oh, hi." The man's voice became friendlier. "Piper was with us tonight, Jack, at a party for our wedding. She lost her cell on the boat. We have it now. My fiancée and I are on our way over to her apartment to drop it off. We'll tell her you called when we see her."

CHAPTER

95

PIPER WATCHED IN stunned silence as Marguerite calmly walked toward the desk. The older woman bent down, opened the bottom drawer, and extracted a gun.

"All right, get up, Piper," said Marguerite, pointing the weapon at her.

"Marguerite, *please*," Piper pleaded. "What are you doing?"

"Do as I say, Piper. Now."

"But, Marguerite, stop and think for a minute," Piper warned, her voice cracking. "You're only going to make things worse."

Marguerite shook her head. "I don't think so, Piper. *You* are the only one who threatens me right now. I think I'll get away with all of it, as long as you don't have a chance to talk to anyone. Now, get up. We're going for a ride."

Piper tried to think. She remembered all the stories her father had told her about murder victims whose fatal mistake had been getting into a car at gunpoint. At the time Piper had vowed she'd never be that stupid. But now, as she stared down the barrel of a gun herself, she understood why the victims had done as they were instructed.

The choices were limited. Try to run and get shot doing it. Try to wrestle the weapon away and get shot doing that. Or follow orders and try to buy precious time. Once they were in the car, she might have more options. She might be able to jump out or signal to another motorist or a pedestrian for help. Right now, alone with Marguerite at the back of the bakery, there was no prospect that anyone would be coming to her aid.

Piper rose from the chair and turned toward the door. Marguerite followed behind her. But Piper's hopes immediately deflated when they got outside to the alleyway. Marguerite clicked the button on her key fob, and the car's trunk lid popped open.

CHAPTER

96

As she stood behind Piper with the gun pointing at her back, Marguerite tried to anticipate what Piper might do. What was she thinking right now?

She must be realizing that getting into the trunk of the car was like signing her own death warrant. Once inside, she could be taken anywhere. Perhaps to some remote spot where she could be killed, the gunshots ringing out where nobody could hear and her body dumped where no one would find it for days and days, if it was ever found at all.

If I were Piper, thought Marguerite, *this is when I'd make my move. I'd take my chances now and run, scrambling down the alleyway as fast as I could, praying that the darkness would make me an elusive target. If I could just get to the end of the alley and out onto the street, I'd have a good chance of survival.*

Before Piper could try any such thing, Marguerite repositioned the weapon in her hand and raised her arm. She brought the heel of the gun crashing down onto Piper's head. The young woman crumpled but didn't completely fall. Yet the blow was enough to daze and destabilize Piper, making it easier to propel her into the trunk.

Marguerite slammed the lid shut and went back inside the bakery to get the computer.

CHAPTER

97

Blackness.

Piper's eyes were open, but she couldn't see anything. Her head throbbed painfully as she struggled to get her bearings. Soon enough she realized what was happening and where she was.

Cramped and barely able to move in the small, cluttered space, Piper raised her arms upward and pressed against the roof. When it didn't move, she clenched her hands into fists and pounded on the unyielding surface. Finally she wriggled around awkwardly and got into a position where she could partially draw up her legs. She pushed her feet as hard as she could against the trunk lid. It did not budge.

Stop. Think. Try not to panic.

Lying in the trunk, trapped and alone in the darkness, Piper could sense her mind racing as a familiar, frantic feeling began to course through her. The trauma, the stress, the sheer terror of her paralysis in Florida and her entombment in the New Orleans movie-set crypt: the sense of being buried alive, caught in a horrific situation from which there was no escape. Helpless.

It was happening all over again!

The terror Piper felt with a flashback was real, but now actual physical threat was imminent. She pictured Marguerite opening the trunk and aiming the gun. She thought of her parents and Jack. She wondered if anyone would ever find her body.

Please, God. Don't let this be happening!

Piper broke out in a cold sweat. She was finding it increasingly difficult to breathe. The short, shallow gasps came faster and faster. She was hyperventilating.

Then she blacked out.

CHAPTER

98

O<small>N</small> R<small>OYAL</small> S<small>TREET</small> the plainclothes police officer took his hand from the pocket of his blazer and looked at his watch with impatience. He was eager for his relief to arrive. Where was the guy?

He was about to call and check when he noticed the lights go off inside the bakery across the street. Wouldn't you know it? Piper Donovan would be coming out any second, heading up to the apartment for the night. The next guy on duty most likely wouldn't have a thing to do for his entire shift. If he were smart, he'd bring a blanket with him and catch up on some sleep in one of the doorways.

Keeping his eyes trained on the front door of the bakery, the man still on duty wondered what Piper had been looking for when she'd come outside earlier. Whatever it was, she hadn't found it. He'd hoped then that she would pack it in for the night.

Here he was, still waiting for a girl he doubted was a threat to anybody. Why hadn't she come out?

Spotting his replacement walking toward him now, the surveillance officer yelled, "You stay here! I'm going to run around and check the back!"

A CAR WAS BACKING OUT of the alleyway. The rear lights flashed brighter red as the driver braked before easing out onto the street. The officer hurried to the car window and held up his badge. He recognized the woman behind the wheel. She looked at him warily as she lowered the window.

"Mrs. Olivier," he said. "Good evening, ma'am."

"What's wrong, Officer?" asked Marguerite.

"I don't mean to worry you, Mrs. Olivier, and I want to offer my deepest sympathies. Your husband made the best beignets in New Orleans, and we both know that's saying something."

Under the lamplight the cop noticed that Marguerite seemed to relax.

"Thank you," said Marguerite. "I hope to have the bakery open again soon. We'll still make Bertrand's recipes. Make sure to come in, and I'll give you some. Good night."

Marguerite took her foot off the brake, and the car began to move.

"Wait a minute, ma'am," he said as he looked into the car and spotted the computer on the backseat. "Have you seen Piper Donovan, the girl who's been working with you? I know she was in the bakery tonight. Do you know where she is now?"

PIPER GROGGILY DRIFTED BACK TO consciousness. Slowly she became seized by the overwhelming feeling that something was wrong. Dreadfully wrong.

Then it came to her what that was. Piper kept her eyes shut tight, as if keeping them closed would somehow block out the horror of what was happening. But the cold fright pulsed inexorably through every fiber of her body anyway.

She could hear the motor running, but the car didn't seem to be moving. Listening closely, she heard muffled conversation.

Someone else was out there!

Summoning all the strength she had left, Piper began screaming and pounding on the roof of the trunk.

"OPEN UP THE TRUNK, MRS. OLIVIER."

Marguerite ignored the command and pressed her foot on the accelerator. The car moved forward, quickly gathering speed.

With just seconds to react, the officer made a decision. He pulled out his weapon and began firing, focusing on the rear tires of the car as it sped away down the street. He prayed his aim would be accurate.

THE CAR WAS MOVING NOW, faster and faster. As she lay cramped and in pain, Piper was terrified as she heard the shots being fired. What if a bullet hit the trunk—and hit *her* as she lay cowering there?

But she was also strangely relieved. No matter what happened, somebody would eventually find her. Even if Marguerite eluded capture right now and took her somewhere to kill her and dispose of her body, Piper's DNA would still be all over the trunk. Whoever was shooting would have a description of the car and, hopefully, could get the plate number. It would be traced to Marguerite. Sooner or later the police would figure out the rest. Jack would be on their backs every step of the way.

There was comfort in knowing that her parents and Jack, as stricken and heartbroken as they would be if she didn't make it, would know what had happened to her.

Keeping her eyes shut, Piper prayed.

"Our Father, who art in heaven—"

Her prayer was cut short. She heard a bullet whiz into the trunk at the same moment she experienced the force of impact as the car crashed.

FRIDAY
MARCH 21

EPILOGUE

A TALL, DARK-HAIRED MAN got out of a taxi at the entrance to the Tulane Medical Center. He paid the driver and quickly walked through the soaring, skylighted lobby. He fidgeted impatiently as he waited his turn at the reception desk.

"Piper Donovan, please."

The receptionist checked the computer and provided the room number.

"Is there a place where I can buy flowers here?" asked Jack as he took the room pass from the receptionist.

She nodded. "There's a gift shop on the second floor of the Aron Pavilion."

Jack hurried away, stopping briefly to buy a bouquet of pink tulips before proceeding to Piper's room. She seemed to be sleeping when he got there. Her face was deathly pale, punctuated by an angry purple bruise on her forehead.

He pulled a chair next to her bed and sat down, reaching out to take her scratched hand in his. Piper's long, tapering fingers wrapped weakly around his hand. Her green eyes slowly opened, and she looked at him. "Jack," she whispered.

He leaned over and kissed her gently. "How's my girl?" he asked.

"My head hurts," she answered softly. She closed her eyes again.

WHILE PIPER SLEPT, JACK WENT out to the nurses' station and asked for a report.

"Are you a relative?" asked the nurse.

"I'm her fiancé," Jack fibbed. He didn't care that he wasn't being exactly truthful. He had to know how Piper was, and he hoped his lie would be true someday anyway.

"She has a concussion from a blow on the back of her head," said the nurse. "Plus, she sustained another hit on her forehead when the car crashed. Fortunately, she doesn't seem to have broken anything, but she has multiple contusions. We'll be watching her for a while to make sure she doesn't have internal injuries."

WHILE HE WAITED BESIDE PIPER'S bed, Jack called her parents, knowing how worried they must be about their daughter. He was the one who had called them the night before and informed them about what had happened. The Donovans immediately announced they would get the next flight down to New Orleans, but Jack had talked them out of that. He was going and would keep them updated on everything.

Keeping his voice low, Jack gave Terri and Vin a report on Piper's medical status. "Everything will be all right," he finished. "With a little luck and a lot of rest, she should be fine. Sore, but fine."

Jack spoke as if he were sure. He had to believe.

KEEPING HIS EYES ON PIPER the whole time, Jack called his New Orleans FBI contact. Investigators were already searching through the bakery computer. Snake supplies and a sales receipt for an albino California king snake had been found in the trunk of Marguerite Olivier's car. The fingerprint discovered in the blood at the first murder scene had now been identified as belonging to Marguerite.

"Her prints weren't in the system till she was booked last night, Jack," said the field agent.

PIPER STILL SLEPT. A NURSE came into the hospital room and checked her pulse.

"How is it?" asked Jack.

"Steady," answered the nurse. "A bit slow, but nothing alarming."

Jack got up and stretched. His stomach was grumbling. He hadn't had anything to eat since the muffin he grabbed as he ran to catch his plane at the airport in New York early that morning.

"Do you think she'll be all right if I run down to the coffee shop and get something to eat?" he asked the nurse.

The nurse nodded. "Sure. Go ahead."

As Jack left the room, he bumped into a red-haired young woman and dark-haired man entering. Though the woman was wearing jeans and a blouse, it appeared she was ready for a special occasion. Her hair and makeup looked as if they had been professionally done, and sparkling earrings dangled from her ears. The man wore a navy suit and pale blue tie. They introduced themselves.

"Oh!" said Jack. "You're the bride and groom!" He reached out, shook their hands, and gave them a quick update on Piper's condition. "I want to thank you again for calling me back from Piper's cell phone last night and letting me know what happened."

Sabrina shook her head. "I'm glad we could do it," she said. "Arriving at the bakery to return her cell phone and finding an ambulance and all the police cars there was so incredibly scary. It was a relief to have someone to call and notify."

The three of them went inside the hospital room and stood at the foot of the bed, watching Piper as she slept.

"Don't you have a wedding to be at?" asked Jack.

"We're on our way, but we wanted to check on Piper first,"

said Leo. He reached into his pocket, took out the iPhone, and handed it to Jack.

Jack looked at Piper again. "When she wakes up," he said, "I know she's going to be worried that she didn't finish your wedding cake."

"Tell her that that's the last thing she needs to be concerned about," said Sabrina.

Leo agreed. "We have a restaurant, Jack. If I can't figure out something, I don't deserve my chef's hat."

In the hospital coffee shop, Jack paid for a chicken-salad sandwich, a bag of chips, and a bottle of iced tea. He took the elevator back upstairs and hurried down the hall to Piper's room. He was just unwrapping his food when two men appeared at the doorway. One carried flowers, the other carried a little boy in his arms. Falkner Duchamps and Wuzzy Queen introduced themselves.

"And this is my son, Connor," said Wuzzy.

"Well, Piper has certainly made some friends in the short time she's been down here, hasn't she?" asked Jack as he patted Connor on the head.

"And who are *you*?" asked Falkner.

"Jack Lombardi, her boyfriend," he answered territorially.

Falkner smiled. "Lucky guy."

"We just wanted to stop by for a minute to make sure Piper was all right," said Wuzzy.

"And I wanted to apologize to her," added Falkner. "I came down on her pretty hard last night on the *Natchez,* and I'm sorry about that now."

Jack shot Falkner a suspicious look, just as there was movement in the bed. All of them turned to see Piper smiling wanly at them.

"Go ahead, Falkner," said Jack. "I guess you can tell her yourself."

FOR THE REST OF THE afternoon and into the evening, Jack sat next to Piper's bed. They talked a little about what had happened on Royal Street, but mostly they spoke about what they would do when they got back home. Piper promised she was going to see a therapist and discuss what she'd been through and the feelings she'd been having.

Piper's parents called several times. And Gabe, her agent, rang to give Piper the positive feedback he'd gotten from the movie people. The casting director wanted to know if Piper would be available for more work sometime in New Orleans. She hesitated a moment before answering.

"Yeah, I mean, for the right role, I'd definitely be willing to come back here. It's such a great city." She never even mentioned to Gabe that she was lying in a hospital bed.

The lines crinkled at the corners of Jack's eyes as he smiled down at her.

THE CAB DROPPED JACK OFF at the hotel on Royal Street. He checked in and dropped his small overnight bag in the room. He was overtired and not ready to sleep.

He decided to take a walk and try to see the places Piper had seen over the past week. He passed by the antique shop and the Gris-Gris Bar. He stopped at Boulangerie Bertrand and peered through the front window. It was dark inside, and he couldn't see much, but he shuddered to think what had gone on there.

A jewelry store, a hat shop, a gift shop, a fortune-telling place. Jack traveled farther along the old lamplit street, thinking about Piper as he went. He stopped at the corner to listen to a musician wearing a porkpie hat as he played "That Old Black Magic" on his clarinet. Jack threw a five-dollar bill into the guy's instrument case and then turned to walk back to the hotel.

THE HOT SHOWER HELPED TO relax him, but Jack still didn't fall asleep right away. He turned on his side, reached over to the bedside table, and switched on the radio. He listened as a series of callers praised the show's host.

"Aaron, the police should hire you, man. You were way ahead of the curve. You called it before anyone else."

"I thought you were crazy, Aaron, when you came up with the hoodoo thing. I thought you were another one of those ego-driven radio hosts, willing to say any outrageous thing just to pump up the ratings. I was wrong."

"I only started listening to your show when I heard about your

Hoodoo Killer theory from a friend of mine. I'm hooked, Aaron, and you'll have another faithful listener from now on. You can count on it."

Jack's phone rang. He turned down the sound on the radio and answered.

"It's me, Jack."

"Hey, you. Everything okay?"

"I can't sleep," answered Piper.

"Me neither," said Jack.

"Thanks for coming down here, Jack," she said softly. "That really means a lot to me."

"And where else would I be? I love you, Pipe."

"I love you, too," Piper whispered. "I can't wait to see you in the morning."

BOULANGERIE BERTRAND BEIGNETS

2 teaspoons dried yeast
½ cup warm water
½ cup granulated sugar
½ teaspoon salt
2 eggs, beaten
2 tablespoons butter, melted and cooled
¾ cup evaporated milk
3 cups all-purpose flour (approximately)
Oil for deep frying
Confectioners' sugar

Makes about three dozen beignets

In a mixing bowl, dissolve the yeast in the warm water. Add the granulated sugar, salt, eggs, butter, and evaporated milk. Mix in enough flour to make a soft but not sticky dough. Knead until smooth and elastic. Leave dough to rise in a warm place until it doubles in bulk.

Punch the dough down and knead again briefly. Roll out to a ¼-inch-thick rectangle. Cut into 3 x 2-inch diamonds. Lay them on a lightly oiled baking sheet, cover, and leave to rise until doubled in height.

Deep-fry in oil heated to 365 degrees Fahrenheit until puffed and golden brown. Drain on paper towels. Serve fresh and warm, sprinkled generously with confectioners' sugar.

Ooh la la!

ACKNOWLEDGMENTS

Mᴀɢɪᴄ. Lᴜᴄᴋ. Pʀᴏᴠɪᴅᴇɴᴄᴇ. I've come to believe that it's the last concept which has influenced the course of my life. Providence defined as God's protective care.

Mostly I've seen examples of Providence in the human beings who have crossed my path at critical junctures. People who provided what I needed when I needed it. People who helped me keep going. People who pointed the way.

Providential creatures have also influenced each book I've written. I've seen them at work again in *That Old Black Magic.*

Father Paul Holmes was there every step of the journey, *providing* support throughout the writing process and sharing his many creative talents. Paul stands, loyal and steadfast. If his is not divine care, I don't know what is.

Elizabeth Higgins Clark, my thespian daughter, *provided* Piper's voice and acting realism. From across the continent, Elizabeth cheered me on.

I'm indebted to Daniel Baum for his reportage in *Nine Lives: Mystery, Magic, Death, and Life in New Orleans.* His vivid

ACKNOWLEDGMENTS

and memorable account of inhabitants of the dazzling, tortured, heroic Crescent City made me even more eager to set my own book there.

For firsthand experience with parenthood and cerebral palsy I turned to my cousin, Colleen Lyons. Thank you, Colleen, for being so open and willing to help me.

Joni Evans gave freely of her formidable talent and precious time: reading, commenting, and suggesting. Her generosity astounds me. It was Joni who led me years ago to agent extraordinaire and now good friend Jennifer Rudolph Walsh. Wow, that was *providential*!

The team at William Morrow/HarperCollins supplied the necessary *provisions*. Editor Carrie Feron, *pro* that she is, offered her savvy ideas to improve the story. Maureen Sugden's fine and expert copyedits were a delight to review. Sharyn Rosenblum and Abigail Tyson are my hardworking and amazing publicity team. Many thanks also to Kimberly Chocolaad, Nicole Fischer, Lynn Grady, Tavia Kowalchuk, Shawn Nicholls, Virginia Stanley, Liate Stehlik, and the many others, unnamed here, who contributed their talents to usher *That Old Black Magic* out into the world.